# THE NEW WORLD STORY OF PUNJABI SUPER HERO

------------------------------------------------------------------

# *[Now → Book 1 = Protect & Survive Earth and Bonus Chapter] ~English~*

## *(Volume – 1)*

---------------------------------------------------------------

*Book 2 = Jade Worrier (Crimson) - Coming Soon...*
*Book 3 = Dark Worrier - Coming Soon...*
*Book 4 = Darkness Return - Coming Soon...*
*Book 5 = Revenge of Darkness - Coming Soon...*

------------------------------------------------------------------

**Author by Harvinder Singh Sandhu**
**Email _ Detective.Har@Gmail.Com**
**YouTube Channel _ DetectiveHar**
**Instagram _ DetectiveHar**

~~~~~~~~~~~~~~~~~~~~~~~~~~~~~~~~~~~~~~~~~~~
~~~~~~~~~~~~~~~~~~~~~~~~~~~~~~~~~~~~~~~~~~~

First, I want to tell you how I thought the story of this book and if you do not want to read it, then you can start reading the story from the next page.

Now if you like Fairy Tales, Mysteries, Comedy, Magic, Science Fiction, Drama, feel like true, etc. then you should read this book. Because maybe in this book you can see the glimpse of all the characters like those cartoons, anime and etc. that you see in childhood or still on TV and I hope you will not be disappointed to read this story.

When I thought about the story. Then I used to watch cartoons a lot since childhood, so maybe I got more thinking power so that I keep thinking in my thoughts. Then I thought about a story in 2012. Which I could give free to any TV channel, comic, or anyone who could reach this story to people all over the world and I had told my story to some people who made Punjabi films in 2012, but nobody published my story. So now, after 8 years, I am self-publishing this book with the help of Amazon Kindle.

How a typical boy living in Goa city becomes a superhero…. ☺

# (Chapter – 1)

## [The Story Begins 1,728,000 Years Ago]

This story begins 1,728,000 years ago. When there were people like honest, virtuous etc. on our earth. At the same time, a big war was going on in a different world of different dimensions. People of different dimensions were coming to our world to avoid war, and the person who created that another world. That person orders his two-special people. When our warriors were going to another world, our warriors were trapped in the time interval and moved 1,728,000 years ahead. Now our warriors 1,728,000 will be born again in the future world. Now both of you will go there and when the right time comes, our warriors has to be reminded of their real work and when all the warriors are found, then tell the truth all of them.

# [Now Present Time]

The special person who has come to remind the warriors of other worlds of different dimensions, their real work, the person talks to his other partner on the phone.

This person = you got someone?

The other person = no, and you?

This person = no! The creator has told us this time. Today we will get the first warrior. However, don't know where he will be?

At the same time, the phone alarm was ringing on the other side. "Ring-Ring-Ring..."

Then HR suddenly wakes up, seeing the time, says that I am late again in going to my work, and says aloud that mother you did not wake me up? HR then quickly prepares to go to his job. After getting ready HR tells his mother = mother I am going to my work, but HR's mother says = wait HR, after eating food you go to work, but HR goes towards his work on his bike Without eating food.

HR goes through an empty road to go to his job so that he is not delayed in going to his job but a person appears on the road who asks for a lift from HR and HR stops to give a lift to the person.

HR = Where do you want to go?

This person = yes, I had to go a little further, would you give me a lift to go a little further?

HR = Okay sit on the bike.

This person = thanks

# [On The Way]

HR = Leave you till where?

This person = just a little way away. By the way, my name is Ravi. What is your name?

HR = my name is Harvinder Singh Sandhu.

Ravi = Wow that is a long name!

HR = Yes, but people who know me call me HR.

Ravi = It is a good nickname and is very easy to speak.

HR = Thank you. Where I want to go to work where do you want to go?

Ravi = Just leave me in this place.

When HR leaves Ravi on his way, then HR goes to his work. Ravi tells his other partner on the phone that I have found that first warrior.

**W**hen HR arrives at his work, he starts talking to his friend that suddenly his boss comes there and says in a loud voice = HR Are you still late at work? What is this? Is this your file? You do not even make a file properly and you come late to work. What should I do for you? I cannot even get you out of work because your father is my old friend. Now I will have to tell your father again that you are not focused on work.

Saying this, HR's Boss goes from his office room.

Now HR does his work in a sad way. Then his friend Ajay comes and talks to him.

Ajay = HR are you sad? Boss scolded you again today. When will you make yourself better?

HR = don't know? I feel that I am the only bad luck in this whole world.

Ajay = Do not be depressed. You are a good person; I think your luck is not bad and I think you do not have the work that you can do well.

HR = do you think?

Ajay = Yes, now let's remove the sadness from the face and bring a smile on your face, otherwise the office girls will consider you as a small child. In addition, you have to be ready today and go to the cinema house in the evening.

HR = No, you go alone today.

Ajay = No, you will go today because today my girlfriend is coming with one of her friends. If you do not go then her friend will not come. If her friend does not come then she will not come also, so you will go today. Anyway, we are sometimes discharged early.

HR = you will kill me today

Ajay = No man, you will have a lot of fun.

HR = OK but I have no money.

Ajay = Do not worry I have made all arrangements.

Other Side - Ever since Kali Yuga has started, evil people from other world of different dimensions have been spreading evil on our earth.

The boss of the bad people was named Victor. He is surprised to see the person who suddenly comes in the area of bad people.

Then Victor's servant asks = Boss! Who is this person and why are you so afraid of seeing this person?

Victor slaps the servant and says = shut up, idiot, you do not know who owns us all and who is the creator of evil, he has made all of evil. His name is Darkness, The King of Darkness and it is not his true form because he has no form. This is the greatest evil of the whole universe.

Saying this, Victor leans in front of Darkness and says = Welcome my Master. Master, why did you suddenly come today? Have we made a mistake? If you had any work, you would have told me that I would have come to you on my own.

Darkness = you shut up and listen, which is a 1,728,000-year-old prophecy, that prophecy talks about seven warriors. Those who will end all evil and one of those warriors will be reminded of their power today. Before the warrior remembers his powers, you send your man and kill that warrior.

Victor = as you wish my Master.

On the other side - after being discharged from work, HR goes to the cinema house with Ajay in Ajay's car.

On reaching the cinema house, Ajay introduces HR to the girls.

HR's heart gets happy by meeting the girls, when they all start watching the film, HR's mind starts getting depressed again. The film was not even half done that HR starts getting up from theaters and then his friend Ajay stops him and says = HR where are you going?

HR = I do not want to watch the film.

Ajay = What? Are you sad with Boss's scolding in the morning? In addition, if you left, what would I tell these girls?

HR = No, I am thinking about my dad and forgive me because now you can say anything to girls but I will not be able to stop anymore.

Ajay = No problem, if you want go, then go and I will tell girls that your health is not good.

HR = Oh thank you

Ajay = Never mind, you go home and relax.

HR = Okay, I'll go.

**N**ow HR starts moving from the cinema house to his house. On the way, HR keeps thinking about his father. On the way HR does not get noticed and he starts walking towards the middle of the road that suddenly a car starts coming towards HR and as the car gets closer to HR, a girl comes running and that girl save the HR by leaping.

Then that girl tells HR angrily = what were you thinking? Don't you see? Do you have eyes on the top?

HR = Hey girl you don't know how upset I am.

Girl = If you are upset, will you walk in the middle of the road?

HR speaks angrily = I just don't want to talk anymore and thank you for saving me.

As soon as HR says this, he goes from there way and that girl speaks while looking at him from behind = there is something different about this boy.

**N**ow as soon as HR reaches his house and opens the door, he is scared to see in front. Because he sees his dad at the door and thinks that, his dad is at home.

Father = HR, how was your day today? Are you having fun at work? Because i got a call from your boss today.

Thinking of HR with anger in mind = Boss! I will see you; you are a very bad boss.

Father speaks angrily = Harvinder; what are you thinking? Where is your attention? You do not do your work properly and do not listen to me properly. Don't know how your future will be? Now today you will not be allowed to come home.

Saying this, HR's Father closes the door of the house.

HR knocks on the door and says = Dad will not do this again.

Then HR goes somewhere after knocking on the door for a while.

**N**ow HR walks down the dark road with a sad face. While walking, he thinks that someone is following him, and then one person comes and stands in front of him. HR gets scared and starts going backwards, then suddenly another person stand backwards also. HR does not see the face of those people because that street was very dark.

HR = who are you, brother?

However, if HR does not get the answer, it becomes even more frightening. Then both of them start coming towards HR when suddenly third another person comes there and starts fighting with first two unknow person. After two minutes of fighting, the two men fled and then that third person tells HR that we should go somewhere else because this place is not safe and then both go somewhere else.

**O**ther side – Both bad people fail and reach their place.

Victor = what is the news? Did that warrior die?

Both bad people speak out of fear = Boss we could not kill him because someone else was there and we could not even see the face of both of them because that was a dark place.

Darkness angrily wipes them both with one finger. In addition, he tells Victor that we had only one chance to see that warrior and die.

Victor speaks fearfully = Boss does not get angry with me, because we can still kill him.

Darkness speaks angrily = No, now you won't be able to kill him and when you had a chance, why didn't you send people with powers?

Victor speaks fearfully = But my boss, I sent two of my best men to die that warrior and boss you told me that the warrior has no power yet.

Darkness = shut up. What did you think that if that warrior does not have any power, then would the warrior who comes to save him also have no power? I have given you so much power and you are using people who do not have power?

Victor = sorry my boss, this mistake will not happen again.

Darkness = Now you send any of your demons in the crowded area because if that warrior has remembered his power then he will definitely come there.

Victor = as you wish my master.

On the other side – HR and that person reach some safe place and HR looking at the person says that you are the one whom I gave lift in the morning and your name is Ravi, am I right.

Ravi = Yes, you are right and sent me to support you because you are the first Red Rainbow warrior. Your soul has come from another world of different dimensions, but that world was being destroyed. Therefore, after coming here on the planet Earth of this dimension, you had to be born again and now you have to save this planet from being destroyed.

HR = Wow, what a good story. You are saying that I am a superhero like Shaktimaan, Superman, or Spiderman and now I have to save this world too. Ha-ha, I think I am having a dream because I was so sad with my father, then by showing me such dreams my brain would be making me happy.

Ravi = this is not a dream and I am not the violence of your dreams because I have come from far away to remind you of your real work.

HR thinks for a moment and then speaks = Why me? Why have

you chosen me?

Ravi = I have not chosen you. Your soul has chosen you. When I saw you this morning, at the same time I came to know that you are the red rainbow warrior because you are very sincere but keep crying like a baby.

HR = Hey, this is happening a lot now. I should think of a way to finish this dream.

Ravi = If you still do not believe it to be true then I give you something.

As soon as he speaks, Ravi holds the hand of HR and brings a bracelet with magic.

Ravi = you wear this bracelet and say this =

**~~ Lightning of Fire gives me power to end the Darkness ~~**

HR speaks wearing a bracelet =

## ~~ Lightning Of Fire Gives Me Power<br>To End The Darkness ~~

## *~~ Transform ~~*

HR is shocked and says = what have I changed? Wow, I really have become like a superhero as are Shaktimaan, Superman, or Spiderman. I think this dream is getting more interesting.

Saying this, a voice is heard to HR. help me - help me and HR says = what is it that I have heard? It sounds like my friend Ajay.

Ravi = you have changed the red rainbow warrior, so you are hearing the voices of people in trouble and now you have to go to save them.

HR = Okay then let us go there.

Here, the demon sent to the cinema house had controlled all the people and was taking the energy of all those people. That is when the sound comes from the door = Leave them all.

Demon = who are you?

Red Warrior thinks; my name.... Then suddenly a voice comes out from inside the warrior.

I am Red Rainbow Warrior. To destroy evil forces. To drive away the darkness. To erase evil from evil people. I have brought the power of truth and goodness. Listen, if evil people want to escape, then leave the evil, otherwise you will end with that evil.

Demon = you have come Rainbow Warrior? I was waiting for you that now nobody can save you from me. Now you have to die.

As soon as the demon says this, the demon sends the controlled people to the warrior. To make the warrior die. The Red Warrior escapes from controlled people and falls down and sits along a wall. Now the Red Warrior starts getting scared and fearfully says that I do not want to see this dream anymore. I want to go home

Demon = you cannot go anywhere because you have to die now.

As soon as the demon says this, the people who are under control start moving towards the warrior and seeing the warrior coming towards him, he is scared and starts crying loudly. Then the warrior's cry produces a dangerous sound wave.

The demon begins to suffer hearing that sound wave and all the people under control faint. Then the demon says loudly = shut up little children.

Hearing this, the warrior becomes silent and sees that all the people controlled have fainted.

Demon = I think you will die by my hands.

Saying this, the demon extended his hand towards the warrior and then suddenly a ray of light "that looks like a rose" strikes the demon's hand and injures the demon's hand. Then everyone looks at that other side. A girl wearing a mask was standing there at the window.

Demon = Now who are you?

Masked girl = I am Mysterious Girl and You're Rainbow Warrior, we were waiting for you to save this world and now you have come, then help me to eliminate evil from this world.

Red Warrior = I do not know how to help you because I do not know how to use my powers.

Mysterious Girl = Never mind if you think about how to use your powers, until then I give you some time by fighting this monster.

Therefore, the Mysterious Girl fights the monster and here the Red Warrior thinks about how he turned into a superhero and while thinking it misses some words. With which it was transformed into a superhero and some of its words are remembered by him, which he repeats = [Lightning of Fire], but nothing happens. Then the Red Warrior feels something from within himself and he repeats the same word again loudly **[Lightning of Fire]** and then the red light comes from the warrior's fingers that hit the demon. Then the demon is destroyed by lightning.

Seeing this, the Red Warrior happily says = I have defeated that monster.

Mysterious Girl = Red Warrior You are very brave, so do not cry anymore like children because this is just the beginning. In future, you have to fight demons that are even more dangerous.

Speaking of this, the Mysterious Girl leaves from there and Here everyone was coming to consciousness.

Seeing this, the Red Warrior also leaves the cinema house. Coming out of the cinema house, the red warrior meets Ravi and goes towards his house.

Ravi = Red warrior It has been quite a night now, so your father will not stop you from coming to your house and now I will see you tomorrow.

Speaking so much, Ravi sees that the Red Warrior was smiling in the memory of someone.

Ravi speaks surprised. = Red warrior you are listening to me? Why is your face red and you knowing how to become an HR back?

Even after hearing this the red warrior only says this = that girl was Very Beautiful.

Other side – Darkness gets the news. Our sent demon is finished by the warrior. Now Darkness tells his servants = that warrior has killed our demon, but now we have come to know how powerful the warrior is and now we have to think how that warrior should die and now those other warriors too must find.

The next day HR is late again to go to work and when HR arrives at work. Then Ajay talks to HR = Hey HR, when you left the cinema house yesterday, a demon came to the cinema house and started controlling everyone. Then a person named Red Warrior comes there and saves the lives of all the people.

As soon as Ajay says this, his boss comes back and Ajay starts doing his work.

Now Boss speaks again to HR = HR you are late again at work and do not do work properly, etc.

HR again apologizes to Boss and says = Boss forgive me, this will not happen again.

However, HR was very happy from now........ :)

## (Chapter – 2)

Now in this city a woman comes in her mini bus, which is a famous astrologer. She parked the mini bus in the street. Now this news spreads throughout the city. Hearing this news, the people of the city come to the woman to get information about his future and in no time, there is a long line of people in front of that woman's mini bus. The same evening a man from Victor sees that line and tells the news to Victor and Darkness.

**D**arkness = we take advantage of this news. Victor, makes our demon such a fake astrologer and set up an astrologer home so that the demon can control all the people who come there. Then everybody will do bad things. Seeing these evil deeds, he and all the other warriors will come to save all those people. Then our demon can kill all those warriors.

Victor = as you wish, my master.

**N**ext day morning - When someone's call was coming on HR's phone, then HR picked up the phone to answer the call, Ravi speaks to HR on the other side of the phone.

Ravi = have you woken up?

HR talks in half sleep = what are you saying?

Ravi = you cannot complete your special work like this.

HR speaks in half sleep = what?

Ravi says loudly = wake up, today you will go to work late, so how will you do your warrior work?

Hearing this, HR wakes up from half his sleep and looking at the time.

HR = what, why don't you call me early? You said you woke me up early today. Nevertheless, I am late again to go to my work.

Ravi = you see well, I have been calling you for the last one hour. I do not know how to change you.

Hearing this, HR disconnects the call, then gets ready quickly and goes towards his work.

When HR arrives at his work, he walks calmly towards his desk, but an office girl named Neha says good morning to HR and this voice is heard to his boss, then his boss scolds HR for arriving late at work and Neha hears scolding with HR.

After being scolded, when the boss goes to his room, HR asks Neha = Neha, why did you also have scolded with me?

Neha speaks blushing = I do not know, maybe it will be difficult for me to explain.

HR = Who cares.

At the launch time office, Neha calls Ajay to ask him something.

Ajay = Here I come. So why did you call me?

Neha speaks blushing = HR is your best friend, so tell me if I ask HR for a date, will he go on a date with me? This will deepen our relationship even further and maybe he marries me in future.

Ajay speaks laughing = It can never happen because HR still thinks like children.

Now Neha gets sad.

Ajay = Forgive me. I think if you go directly from the front and ask him, he probably say yes.

Neha = so I ask him from behind.

Ajay = No, no, no, I did not mean that. I am saying that you go to some astrologer and ask him what you should do next. In addition, I have heard that today a new astrological house has opened in the city and I have also heard that people were saying that the astrologer there tells very bright future. Now you go there after work and ask them your future. Okay.

After the job, HR goes on the woman, who had come to the city a day earlier to tell the future. Then he sees that the long line in front of that woman's mini bus is not there today. Therefore, HR goes to that mini bus to talk to the woman = Hello ma'am, you are a very famous astrologer, so why are there no people in front of your mini bus today?

That woman speaks with a smile = Because there is a new astrological house open on the front side today and the one who told the future has come true, but I think that the astrologer who tells the future makes it true himself.

HR speaks on seeing that new astrologer's house = I feel bad from inside. What will you do now?

That woman = people always need something new in this world.

HR = I know what you will do. You can tell my future by looking at my hand.

That woman = Thank you son, I am seeing a girl in your future who likes you. She always sees you all the time.

HR = Really? Thank you.

Saying this, HR comes out of the mini bus, and then HR thinks who can be the girl who likes me? Therefore, HR thinks maybe it is Ritu who runs the coffee shop I visit often.

So, HR goes to that coffee shop and suddenly a voice comes from behind = Hello HR, you have not seen for two days.

HR = Oh! Ritu, you scared me.

Ritu = Why are you scared like children all the time? Why are you standing outside now? Let me give you a new type of coffee, which has come to my shop this morning.

HR = Thank you.

Now HR was going to mix coffee with milk that Ritu comes to him and asks = you tasted coffee?

HR = No, just mix a little milk and then taste it.

Ritu = Give me, I help you.

Ritu helps HR by speaking it. Then HR thinks in his mind = I am nervous but I am happy.

Then Ravi stands on the side, who looks at HR and says = HR, why is your face red?

So, HR gets shocked and says = Ravi you?

Ravi speaks smilingly = O ho someone feels loved?

Ritu = you are Ravi. Nice name. Our name is very similar.

Ravi = Oh yes.

HR speaks angrily = Why have you come?

Ravi = you do not know we have to do something special?

Ritu = special work? What is that special work and can I help you to do that work?

Ravi = Yes, of course...

HR stops Ravi's talk and speaks up = not at all. Excuse me because that particular work is secret and only a select few can do it. Ravi now you go with me and do that special work.

Saying this, HR starts leaving that place and Ritu stops HR and says = you did not drink your coffee.

HR = sorry I will come again.

Ritu = Ok, so I will wait for you. Because I like when I see your face.

HR speaks blushing = Thank You.

Speaking of this, HR and Ravi come out from the coffee shop.

Now HR speaks to Ravi = Why did you come? You know what a good time it was going.

Ravi = you should not stop anywhere on your way home.

HR = Yes, this is not good thinking.

Ravi = finally you understand. Now you can start doing that special work.

HR = Why not.

Speaking of this, HR starts going somewhere with Ravi.

Ravi = Where are we going?

HR = I have to ask that future woman about Ritu.

Speaking of this, when HR and Ravi reach the place where the woman's mini bus was, HR sees that the woman and her mini bus are not there.

HR = I am too late. What do I do now?

Now HR thinks in his mind seeing that astrological house = still I want to know the future right now. Nevertheless, should I go to this place? However, I do not feel good seeing this.

Ravi = HR what are you doing? In addition, why are we standing in front of this astrological house?

HR = nothing, nothing.

Then suddenly HR thinks = I know what to do. I should ask my future to myself. Now I jump my shoe upwards and if the shoe falls on the upper side, then I will go to this astrological house and if the shoe falls upside down, I will go back to my house.

When the HR shoe bounces up, the shoe hits a girl's head. So, HR looks at the girl and says = this is the girl who saved me from hitting the car.

Now that girl comes towards HR and says = you don't see? Eye on top.

HR speaks angrily = Do not call me by this name.

That girl = it hurts. If you had a girlfriend, you would probably have the ability to talk to girls.

HR says angrily = thanks for giving me my shoe.

Saying this, HR and Ravi go away from there and HR tells Ravi on the way = that girl turned off my mood.

**N**ow HR and Ravi were going on the road, HR heard a voice = Hey HR! Then HR looks here-there and then his mother sees him on the way.

Then HR goes to his mother and says = Mom, have you come to buy something?

Mother = Yes, your father was home early today, so he was saying that today he makes something special to eat. Therefore, you want to eat something special.

HR thinks in mind = I am sure Ritu will like mother.

Mother = HR, you should not roam this way after work and who is with you?

HR = Oh I am sorry. This is my friend Ravi.

Ravi = Glad to meet you.

Now they all go home.

Mother = Me too.

**O**ther side - when HR and all the employees are discharged from work, then Neha and some other girls who work with HR. She all moved into that new astrological house. In addition, there too many people came to know their future. Now the man who was telling the future was actually a demon of darkness. The demon was controlling all the people one by one. When Neha starts asking her future to that demon, the demon asks her to sit with him. The demon then tells Neha to look into his eyes. Then the demon takes Neha under his control and says = Now you are all under my control. You are now servants of all evil. Now you all have to forget all your work and do bad things. Hahaha...... very soon evil will spread in this world.

**N**ext day - Today HR has arrived early at work. Then Ajay starts talking to HR = HR, did you talk to Neha yesterday?

HR = what are you talking about?

Ajay = you do not know that Neha likes you but she is shy to tell you.

HR = what are you talking?

Then a voice comes from behind = Hello HR, let us go on a date.

HR = what happened to you, Neha? Why are you wearing party dresses?

Neha speaks by holding HR's hand = Do not waste my time by talking about this idle. Now you give me a kiss.

After saying this, Neha starts kissing HR; HR gets scared and starts shouting loudly. After hearing this noise, his boss comes. Now the boss speaks = Why is this noise made? What are you all doing and Neha, why have you come wearing this party dress?

Now Neha gives no reply to the boss and slaps the boss. Then the boss gets angry and slaps Neha. Therefore, another office girl strikes the head of the boss with something and the boss faints. Now all the girls left the office, which was under the control of the demon. Then comes the news from the city that many people of the city are sabotage like crazy. Now Ajay tells HR = When I spoke to Neha yesterday, she wanted to take you on a date. Then I asked Neha to go to that new astrologer's house so that Neha could know her future to take you on a date. Now today Neha does not know what has happened.

HR = I have to go.

He leaves the office after speaking. Now on the way HR meets Ravi and Ravi tells HR = All these people are under control of evil.

HR = Ajay told me about that new astrological house. Our office girls and all the people who went to that astrological house, they all those people have started doing bad things.

Ravi = you are right.

HR = Now you will give me some other superhero thing in gifts?

Ravi = No it cannot be right now. Now you change into a rainbow warrior, then go to that new astrologer's house and finish that evil and save all those people who are under the control of that evil.

HR = Okay so now I turn into Rainbow Warrior. However, I forgot how I had changed before?

Ravi = Oh how forgetful you are? Speak with me: -

**~~ Lightning of Fire gives me power to end the Darkness ~~**

HR = OK.

## ~~ Lightning Of Fire Gives Me Power To End The Darkness ~~

## *~~ Transform ~~*

**O**ther side – the demon in the new astrologer's house talks to the controlled people and says = you all did a great job. Especially you girls. Now the time has come for me to control the whole city and spread evil so that my boss will be happy and make me more powerful. Now suddenly the door of the astrologer's house opens and a person stands in front of the light coming from outside and says this = that woman was right. You are spreading evil in this city by controlling all these people by telling them their wrong future. I will not let all this happen.

Demon = who are you?

Red Warrior = I am Rainbow Red Warrior. To destroy evil forces. To drive away the darkness. To erase evil from evil people. I have brought the power of truth and goodness. Listen, if evil people want to escape, then leave the evil, otherwise you will end with that evil.

Demon = Oh, you have come, rainbow warrior. My boss told me that you would definitely come to save all these people. Now you will die, you cannot escape from my attack.

Red warrior survives the attack and says = hey you are cheating; I was just talking and you should give a speech for some evil? Because this happens in all stories.

Demon = There is no time for all these useless things. You all finish that warrior.

Now all the controlled people go towards the warrior to die and the red warrior sees all those people coming towards him and says this = You are all under the control of that demon right now. You all stop now because I do not want to harm you all.

Nevertheless, those controlled people do not stop and when they are about to attack the warrior, suddenly a light ray that looks like a rose comes from the other side and hits the demon nose and the demon Control loses from all those people.

Seeing the other side, the demon comes in his real form and says = who is interfering in this fight.

Red warrior sees all those people frozen and looking at the other side, he says = you have come here, Mysterious Girl.

Mysterious Girl = Red Warrior, do not think how hard it will be. Just trust yourself and you can defeat all these evil. So now, you can kill this demon alone. Now we will meet again.

Saying this, the Mysterious Girl leaves and seeing the Mysterious Girl go, the Red warrior smiles and says this = Thank you very much Mysterious Girl.

Now the demon makes many attacks on the Red Warrior. However, the Red Warrior, while avoiding that attack, remembers the attack from which he killed that first demon. Then the

Red Warrior speaks those words to start that attack = **(Lightning of Fire)** but nothing happens.

Demon = Rainbow warrior, you cannot kill me by saying anything.

Then the red warrior thinks in his mind = Mysterious Girl told me I should trust myself only then I will be able to eliminate all these evil. Now I should say those words again with my whole faith and then that attack will start so that I can defeat this demon.

Now the Red Warrior starts to trust himself completely, he realizes the power that Ravi was talking about, then he speaks those words aloud **[Lightning of Fire]**, then that attack hits the demon and that demon dies. Then all those people who were under the control of that demon, they all get well. Now seeing this, the red warrior says to all those people = you all take care of yourself.

Saying this, the Red Warrior leaves from there. Now coming out of that place, the red warrior meets Ravi and changes into HR.

Ravi = you have been able to beat today's demon very hard.

HR = Yes forgive me because I forgot my attack.

Ravi = No, you did not forget your attack. Rather you did not trust your powers due to which you were not able to start your attack.

HR = Oh, forgive me; I will now trust my powers.

Ravi = don't worry. You will all learn very soon. Now you should go to your home.

HR = Yes Okay.

Having said this HR goes to his house.

**N**ow on the other side - Victor realizes that the warrior has killed his demon. Now Victor thinks, how I tell it to Darkness.

**N**ext Day Morning – outside the office, Ajay meets Neha and says this = Yesterday you and other office girls had misbehaved with the boss and you even tried to kiss HR. Then you and other office girls, along with some people, did some bad things in the city.

Now Neha is shocked to hear this, then starts crying and speaks while crying = it is all wrong. Now what about me? Do I have to quit my job now? Now everyone will call me a bad girl.

Ajay = Neha, don't you worry because this morning there was news in TV that the new astrological house was opened in the city. First, the owner of that astrological house controlled all the people who came there and then after that he did bad things in the city with all the people. Now that person and his astrological house have both disappeared.

Saying this; A voice comes from behind Neha = Good Morning.

Neha gets nervous after seeing HR and she says = Oh HR forgive me for tomorrow's bad behavior.

HR = Never mind because it happened yesterday, I have forgotten it.

Neha = Thank you. You have forgotten about yesterday. I need to be more like you. Like you come to the office late every morning and then after coming, the boss scolds you and you don't do your job properly. Despite all this, you still forget.

Saying this, Neha goes inside the office with Ajay.

Now HR speaks angrily = you don't know the trouble I go through.

Speaking of this, HR sees that it is time for the office to start. Then quickly the HR falls down while going inside the office. Then HR says to himself = Why does this always happen to me...... :(

## (Chapter – 3)

Now Victor goes to his boss Darkness, then Darkness asks Victor = what happened to our plan in which we eliminate the rainbow warriors.

Victor = Leave it all to me, my boss, because I have thought of a new plan, so that we will increase our powers with the chi energy of the people of this world. Then we can finish those rainbow warriors very easily.

Darkness = so what is your plan, Victor?

Victor speaks with a smile = in this world, which everybody wants very much. **{The Love}**

**T**he other side at night - HR was watching TV until late night because HR had come to know that in a new TV program, which comes at night, we could send our letter and choose our girlfriend. Now the program begins. Ajay was also watching this program.

Host of the program = Welcome all of our viewers to this new show called **"Feel the Love"**. In which all of you can send your love letters and we will search for your true love and meet you. It is now midnight and now we are going to choose today's lucky love letter. Therefore, the person who sent today's lucky love letter is Mr. Steve Saxena.

HR speaks surprised = what! Boss? I thought they were married, but this old man is still looking for his girlfriend.

Host of the program = Now we will send a romantic award to this chosen person and search for his girlfriend and when we find that true girlfriend, we will call them both in our TV show and meet them both. Now all I will say to all you lovers is that if you also want to find your true love and want romantic rewards then send us your love letters. Now the TV program is over.

Now HR calls Ravi and Ravi picks up the phone and asks HR with surprise = HR, why did you call me so late at night? Have you come to know of any evil power?

HR = Oh no, I just had to ask you that the new program comes on TV at night. In that program, I want to send a letter and will you help me in writing that letter?

Ravi speaks angrily = did you call me at midnight to write a letter? You do not know how much I was worried and I was thinking that bad people have recognized you.

HR = OK so now will you help me in writing the letter?

Ravi = Forget it! Because you should not run away from your destiny and do not forget that you are a Rainbow Warrior.

HR now speaks angrily = I know, and if you did not want to help me, you would have refused straight away and thank you for giving such a long speech. Good Night. Spoiled the whole mood.

Saying this, HR disconnects the phone and starts sleeping.

**N**ext day morning - Today again HR wakes up late to go to work and when HR arrives at his work, he sees that his boss will probably be late in office today. Now it was one o'clock in the afternoon but his boss had not come to the office yet, so Ajay went to HR and asked him = HR, you know why the boss did not come to the office today?

HR = No,

Ajay = you know, the boss never takes leave for office and never comes late.

As soon as Ajay says this, his boss comes to the office and all the office people see that the boss is very tired and the boss is looking very weak. Now his boss asks all the people in tired condition that one of you who have not worked should raise his hand. Saying this, the boss goes to his room and falls asleep. However, before going to the boss's room, HR's eye goes over the boss's coat, on which was a very beautiful brooch with a black heart shape.

Neha = Let us all go to the boss to see what has happened to them.

HR = you are joking, Neha. You do not think the boss should relax and we have fun.

Neha = No, we should see that the boss does not die due to poor health.

HR = I wish he died.

Neha = What?

HR = No, just kidding.

Now everyone goes to the boss's room and tries to wake them up but the boss does not wake up, then the office people call the ambulance and then the ambulance takes his boss to the hospital.

Ajay = HR, what do you think happened to the boss?

HR = who knows because I never saw the boss sleeping in the office.

Ajay = I think maybe the boss was watching TV until late last night, that is why his health has deteriorated.

HR = you mean the **"Feel the Love"** program that came on TV yesterday at midnight?

Ajay = Yes.

Neha = what are you two talking about and what is this **"Feel the Love"** program?

HR = Hey nothing, just a new program was coming on TV last night. In which anyone can find a lover by sending a letter.

Neha = It will be a very fun program.

HR = Yes, of course, and the boss too was watching that program until late at night, so he is probably getting so much sleep now.

Neha and Ajay = mm maybe.

HR = I just know that now all of us have been discharged today and now I can go home and have fun. ☺

Neha and Ajay = What.

**O**n the other hand, at the TV station the owner of the station asks his employee = what is it? Which program letters are we getting? Because we are not running this program at all, then why are we getting letters of this program?

Employee = Forgive me Boss. I think it is coming by mistake.

Station owner = so fix this mistake now.

Employee = as you wish. I will fix this mistake now boss.

Then there comes a woman who is a demon sent by Victor. She also wore the same black brooch that HR's boss wore and she says = did people send this letter after seeing the new program?

Station Owner = who are you, who let you come in and how could you get a new program without my permission?

Female demon = I tell everything just look in my eyes.

Saying this, the Female demon started to control the station owner and all the employees of the station.

**N**ow on this side, HR and Ajay came together to market and both of them were talking about something on the way.

Ajay = Hey HR you know I have also sent a letter in the **"Feel the Love"** program.

HR = any girl likes you easily and some of them like you, so why did you need to send a letter to that program?

Ajay = That is correct, but I was thinking that my letter would be so special that the people of that program called me there so that girls from all over the city started liking me and I want that romantic reward too.

HR = you are so intelligent. Why didn't I get this idea?

Now HR thinks in his mind that even if he writes the letter...., then HR attention is removed from the front and he collides with someone and he starts apologizing without seeing it.

Ajay = HR, she is a girl and how beautiful. What is your name beautiful girl?

Girl = my name is Rosella! Hey, you are that top-eyed boy. You still haven't learned walking in front of you.

HR said angrily = First do not call me with such a name and second my name is Harvinder Singh Sandhu but my friends call me HR. Okay.

Rosella = so you are HR and still you do not know how to talk to girls. That is why perhaps nobody is your girlfriend yet. If it were, she would have taught you to talk with girls. Hahaha See you again, Eye on Top.

Ajay = what a brave girl and you can take inspiration from this to write your letter.

HR said very angry = this girl, whenever I meet her, it spoils my whole mood and you are saying she can inspire me.

Ajay = Yes.

HR = No, I don't get any inspiration from a girl like this.

**N**ow HR goes to home. When HR reaches home, he sees that Ravi has come to his house.

HR = When did you come?

Ravi = just now.

HR = let's go to my room.

Now HR angrily tells Ravi = will you help me write the letter? Because I want to teach that girl a lesson.

Ravi = which girl?

HR = the one who meets me on the road every day by mistake.

Ravi = Leave it, now what will happen with anger.

HR = No, let me focus on writing.

Ravi = But listen, HR.

HR says loudly = shut up and let me concentrate on writing.

Now Ravi fell silent for a moment and then said this = HR, why are you wasting your time writing this?

HR = you are right I should not write this. Rather, I should go straight to the TV station and speak my mind think to them.

Ravi said in shock = what?

HR = let's go to the TV station.

HR speaks so much and walks towards the TV station.

**N**ow on reaching the TV station, HR realizes that no program like "Feel the Love" program is operated from this TV station. However, HR repeatedly speaks to Security Guard = I know, a program called "Feel the Love" operates from this TV station.

Now the Security Guard speaks with anger = I have told you a thousand times that no such program is operated from this TV station. Now you go to your home.

Ravi = let's go, HR.

HR = Ok I'm going, but I'll solve this mystery.

**N**ow HR and Ravi come home and tonight Ravi stops at HR's house. Now both of them wait for that program to start. When that program starts HR says this = I knew it, this program operates from this TV station and that security guard knows nothing.

Ravi = Wait HR, see this I have searched all over the internet and have seen this TV station website, but I have not been able to find anything about this program. Don't you think something is wrong with this program?

At the same time, the host of that program on TV says this = Now is the time to choose our lucky letter and the person who sent this lucky letter is Mr. Ajay.

HR = It cannot be. Ajay's idea worked.

Host of the program = Now all you lovers listen to me. If you want to get such a reward. So just, send us your letter. We will choose the person sending a letter every night and we will send this reward to that person.

Saying this, this program ends.

Ravi = we see tomorrow what is wrong with this program but we should sleep now.

HR = OK.

**T**he next day morning HR reaches the office and sees that his boss has not come to the office even today and he asks Neha = Neha, why did Bose not come to the office today?

Neha = Boss has not been recovered yet, so the boss still did not come to office.

At the same time, Ajay comes to the office and tells everyone that he has received a reward from the **"Feel the Love"** program.

On seeing the reward, HR forgets that Ravi had last night asked to be alert and tells Ajay to open quickly this prize box. When Ajay opens this prize box, HR looks at this reward and says = Hey, I saw exactly this brooch on the boss's coat.

Ajay = must have seen, but this brooch will look better on me.

Saying this, Ajay wears this brooch on his shirt. Then suddenly Ajay starts sleeping and after saying that I am very sleepy then falls asleep.

Then HR tells Ajay to wake up = Ajay what happened to you? Why are you sleeping, hey Ajay ... Ajay... Ahmm...?

Speaking of this, HR goes so close to Ajay's brooch that he also falls asleep. Now everyone in the office gets scared and starts talking to each other that they should call the doctor and some people say that they should call the police but Neha is very scared to see this and she quickly calls the ambulance is. Now the ambulance takes Ajay and HR to the hospital.

Now HR is in a beautiful place and he sees that Mysterious Girl is standing in front of him, then HR asks him = Hey Mysterious Girl what are you doing?

However, the Mysteries Girl does not say anything. Then she goes to HR and says = Kiss me but HR starts to blush and then he goes to the Mysterious girl's face to kiss her, then suddenly he wakes up from sleep and seeing Ravi near his face, He shouts and says = what are you doing and where is the Mysterious Girl

Ravi = what are you doing? I told you to be alert.

Now Ravi points towards Ajay and says = you are not alert so now see what has happened.

HR = what happened to Ajay and where are we?

Ravi = we are in the hospital and Ajay is controlled by the evil demon with this brooch.

HR = this is easy. We remove this brooch.

Ravi = No, don't do it, otherwise I don't know what will happen. Ajay may sleep forever.

HR = so what should we do now?

Ravi = we have to go to that TV station tonight and finish that monster so Ajay and your boss can survive.

HR = OK.

Now at night Ravi and HR come to the TV station. Therefore, HR sees that he is the same guard who stopped me yesterday.

HR = So, maybe it will not let me go inside the TV station.

Ravi = Okay I understood. Wait I give you something.

Then Ravi closes the eye by holding HR's hand and then HR gets a ring. Now Ravi says = You wear this ring and say **"Power Hidden"** and talk about the body of any human being and you will change into another human being for some time. With this, the demon will not feel your powers.

HR = wow that's good. Okay **"Power Hidden"** Turn Me into A Big Artist.

### ~Transform~

Ravi = what! Bappi Lehri? Is this why you have turned into a big fat person?

HR = Hey I thought a great artist.

Ravi = Never mind, now we should go inside.

HR = Hey Ravi won't you change into another human being?

Ravi = No because I told you on the first day that this is not my real form and real name.

HR = Oh.

Ravi = Now just don't waste much time and let's go inside.

HR = OK.

Ravi = Will you be able to walk in this form?

HR = Absolutely. Look at this.

When HR moves, it falls because of its more stylish appearance.

Ravi = Oh no, I had expected too much. No problem, let's go.

Now, as a famous artist, the guard does not stop HR from entering, so both of them go inside.

**H**ere, other side, inside the TV station, Victor had already come to meet his demon and tells his demon = this method is very good. By this, we can capture the soul of any person and take power from his chi energy. This will make our evil immortal in the whole world Hahaha....

Demon = Yes boss and now it's time to start the program.

Victor = Sure.

Now by starting the program, the demon tells everyone on TV

= Today on this platform a special person who will inform you about our program. His name is Mr. Victor.

Everyone welcomes Victor by cheering.

Victor = Welcome to all our lovebirds on this platform. From tonight, we will choose two people every night to give that special reward.

Here HR and Ravi were watching from outside the recording room that the demon would control two people every night from today.

HR = Look at everyone; they are recording with their eyes closed. It seems that all these people are sleeping. Nevertheless, how is this possible?

Ravi = look closely. These people are really sleeping because this demon has kept all these people under his control.

HR = Okay then I should go inside now.

As soon as HR says this, he starts going inside the recording room, then Ravi speaks while stopping him = Wait now is not the right time. However, HR does not listen to Ravi and goes inside the recording room.

Now HR on stage tells all the audience = you all stop watching this program because this program is a hoax. In this, not all you people will get any lover and all of you will always be alone with this reward. With which you will never be happy. Therefore, you should stop watching this program.

Victor said angrily = what did you do. You ruined my whole plan.

As soon as Victor says this, suddenly demon comes to HR to die, then quickly Ravi speaks to HR = HR look behind you someone is coming towards you.

Then HR escapes from that monster and comes out of the room. Now Ravi and HR go to the top of the TV station but the demon is chasing them.

On reaching the top, Ravi speaks = Right now HR, you should change to Red warrior.

And here HR speaks quickly =

## ~~ Lightning Of Fire Gives Me Power To End The Darkness ~~

# ~~ *Transform* ~~

Now the demon reaches the top and the Red Warrior speaks.

I am Rainbow Red Warrior. To destroy evil forces. To drive away the darkness. To erase evil from evil people. I have brought the power of truth and goodness. Listen, if evil people want to escape, then leave the evil, otherwise you will end with that evil.

Ravi = was it necessary to speak?

HR speaks with a strange face = I do not speak. Just comes from inside.

Demon = you are so weird. Now you have to die.

Saying this, the demon attacks the Red Warrior and quickly Ravi says = Red Warrior, use your powers.

Red warrior quickly speaks with a feeling of heart = **[Lightning of Fire]**

As soon as this is done the red colored laser comes out from the fingers of the red warrior, which goes towards the demon, but if the demon survives this attack, then the red warrior concentrates on that lightning laser, then that power rotates back and strikes the demon. Now the demon is Destroyed.

Seeing this, Victor says = you will die by my hands now.

Red Warrior = Hey another demon?

Victor = I am not a demon, but I am the owner of all these demons and my name is Victor.

Red warrior = your name is Victor or whatever. If I terminate you, all these demons will cease.

By speaking this, the Red Warrior attacks Victor = **[Lightning of Fire]**

Nevertheless, nothing happens to Victor. Then the Red Warrior does Boxing with his hands but still nothing happens. For example, Victor's power is 100% and Red Warrior's power is 10%.

Seeing this, the Red Warrior starts to get scared. Now Victor moves towards the Red Warrior, saying that now you have to die, then suddenly a light ray that looks like a rose comes from the other side, comes, and hits the ground in front of Victor's steps.

Victor = Now I have to go, but the rainbow warrior we will meet again.

Saying this, Victor disappears from this place. Now the red warrior sees the other side. On that side, stood the Mysterious Girl, who left the place calling the Red Warrior Good-Bye.

Ravi = Red warrior, now you should go home because it is too late and your friend, boss and all the people whom the demon had controlled, all are well.

Nevertheless, the red warrior speaks on seeing the Mysterious Girl = this is the queen of my dreams.

Ravi = O red warrior, are you even listening to me?

The next day in HR's office, HR was writing something, then suddenly Ajay comes and snatches the paper from HR and says = Hey HR why are you blushing so much and what are you writing? Is this a love letter? [My dear Mysterious Girl...]

HR = Oh no, don't read this, it's nothing.

At the same time, his boss also comes to the office and speaks = How are everyone. Did you miss me? Because I have missed all of you guys and I am very happy to see you all smiling face.

Here HR speaks to Ajay = this is nothing, just my office work.

Boss = What! HR your office work? Office work completed today. Show me.

Then HR takes the paper from Ajay and speaks to the boss, "Oh no boss, it's nothing and then HR runs to the outside, then his foot hits the table, so, that he falls and paper flies into the air and HR speaks." = Why does this always happen to me?  :(

*(Chapter – 4)*

One-night HR was sleeping and he dreams about how thin he is and everybody was mocking him, then HR suddenly wakes up.

**O**ther side – Darkness confirms with Victor = Victor what is the news?

Victor = very good news.

Darkness = very good then tell me what happened to that warrior?

Victor = my master, the last time I faced that warrior myself. That warrior does not have the strength to fight with us and now I have put fear of weakness through the dreams of people. Now we can lure people to increase their strength and take their chi energy.

Darkness = very good but warrior is also gradually becoming stronger. Therefore, that warrior has to be finished soon.

Victor = as you wish my boss.

**T**he next day, HR, Ajay and his two friends were talking about HR work.

The first friend tells everyone = I have started a workout at home to build my body. So, another friend says = you have benefited from exercising at home? However, I do not see that you will have any benefit. So, the first friend says = you shut up and see you will see a difference in a few days. So, Ajay speaks = what are you saying? You don't have a girlfriend, so why are you both exercising and building your body? So, HR speaks = No Ajay you think if we exercise then firstly our body will be good and then we will be healthy as well which can make our life even longer.

Ajay = Yes, it can happen, that's why the boss is looking so healthy.

HR speaks while laughing = but still he does not find any girl.

Then Neha comes to them and says = Hey guys, do you want to know the secret of being fit for the boss? Wait, I see you something, here are some photos of the boss, which I have saved with the boss's Facebook ID. This is the first photo taken of the boss ID a week ago. How fat is the boss in this and this is another photo I took yesterday from the boss's ID. The boss is now looking healthy.

Ajay = I also heard that the boss is going to the gym for a week.

HR = Ok Neha, so you know the boss is going to the gym from the corner?

Neha = Yes, of course.

Now, HR, Ajay, and his two friends go to the gym together after leaving from work. On reaching the gym, they all get their names registered.

Here someone speaks by looking at HR and their friends = very good, the more people, the more energy we will get.

Now after registration, the host of the gym comes and says = Hello my name is Mr. V and I will tell you all the new ways of exercising today. So, let's start exercising.

Now everybody starts exercising and the people of the gym were helping all the people to exercise, but no one knew that Mr. V is a real Victor who wants to take his chi energy from all these people.

Now after about one and a half hours HR get a call from home, then he goes away telling his friends that he has received a call from home and now he has to go home.

Now when HR reached home, he was feeling very weak, so his younger sister named Harman. She jokingly asks HR = O HR what has happened to you? You look even thinner than before. Has any girl beat you up?

HR speaks angrily = O what are you saying. Mother, make it silent otherwise I will beat it a lot.

Mother = when will you two learn to live together?

HR = First you ask Harman to talk to me properly and I am very hungry. Give me a food.

**T**here had been about two and a half hours in the gym. Now Mr. V says to all the people = Very good, all of you guys have done a very good workout today and now you can all come to this room and relax in this hot water pond because this service is absolutely free.

Now everyone sits in that hot water pond and Victor speaks in his mind = Now we will get a lot of energy.

When everyone takes a bath from that hot water pond, they ask Mr. V = Mr. V we are feeling very weak.

Mr. V = don't worry. This is simply because all of you have exercised for the first time today and now all of you should eat something at home.

Everyone = Okay Mr. V Now we go to our house.

Now when everyone goes to their house, Victor talks to himself = All this human being, everyone is so stupid. They do not know at all that I am taking the chi energy of all these people. Hahaha……

**N**ext day - HR was eating a lot since morning. Nevertheless, even if HR's appetite was not getting over, HR goes to Ritu's café after being discharged from work. When HR reaches Ritu's cafe, Ritu asks HR = Hey HR do you want to eat something?

HR = Yes Ritu but I do not have enough money to satisfy my hunger because this morning I am feeling so hungry that I did not spend my whole life.

Ritu = Oh, so what did you do yesterday that makes you so hungry today?

HR = that I started going to the gym yesterday and since then I am feeling very hungry.

Ritu = Never mind, as long as you are going to the gym, I will pack many launches for you.

HR speaks with feeling = Ritu how good you are.

Ritu speaks with a smile = Oh... thank you very much.

**N**ow HR was walking on the road while eating samosa, then he heard a voice = O "Eye on Top" Then HR looked backwards and there he saw Rosella, who was wearing party clothes.

HR = Oh you are and I have told you how many times do not call me by this name.

Now Rosella smiles and speak to HR = I should not call you "Eye on Top", Rather i should call you "Eye on Food" because now your eyes are only towards food.

HR speaks angrily = when will you improve, crazy girl.

Rosella = you need to improve, "Eye on Food"

Now HR angrily throws Samosa towards Rosella and says = you go away from my eyes.

Then Rosella catches the samosa and it goes away saying = you will never improve. We will meet again "Eye on Food" and thank you for this samosa. Now I have something to eat before going to the party. Bye.

Here Ravi speaks = How much will you fight this girl?

HR speaks with surprise = you are following me?

Ravi = Yes.

HR = How long have you been following me?

Ravi = When you got out of Ritu's cafe, I was behind you ever since.

HR = so why didn't you meet me before?

Ravi = because I was seeing how much you are eating today.

HR = Yes, of course.

Ravi speaks while laughing = If you eat this, much then you will look like a sumo player.

Now HR speaks angrily = you are also making fun of me?

Ravi = Oh no, I am telling the truth. Let's go to some quiet place first.

**N**ow HR and Ravi come to a park.

Ravi = Now tell me how much food you have eaten since this morning?

HR = Let me think. I ate ten loaves before going to work in the morning, and then ate the launch of all my friends at work, and then Ritu gave me a lot of food.

Ravi = so this is too much food for any common person. Now tell me where did you go after work yesterday?

HR = Yesterday I and my friends all went to a gym to workout.

Ravi = I was thinking that there is something wrong, that's why you are eating so much and if you continue to eat like this, you will become very fat very soon.

Now HR gets very nervous and starts thinking in mind = Oh no what should I do now? Because earlier I was thin and now, I will be fat? Don't know when my body will be perfect and fit?

Ravi = you know HR? Now we should check that gym and find out what is wrong.

Nevertheless, HR was not listening to Ravi and he was thinking that when will he be able to take care of his body? So, Ravi speaks loudly = you are also listening to me?

But, HR starts going towards the gym by saying this = I don't want to hear you anymore. Now I have to digest all the food I had eaten since morning and make my body healthy.

So, Ravi speaks to stop HR = it is time to work as a rainbow warrior.

Nevertheless, HR does not stop and speaks while leaving = not yet because I have to exercise now.

Now HR reaches the gym and starts exercising hard and Ravi follows him to the gym. On reaching the gym, Ravi looks inside the window that HR is working very hard and thinks in his mind = when will this boy improve?

Then Ravi's eyes are seen by someone and after seeing him, he speaks to himself = this is the boss of HR, Mr. Steve Saxena and he is looking very weak. As if he is about to die. Nevertheless, where is he going? I should follow them.

Now Ravi chases Steve. So, he sees that someone is taking

Steve to a room and when Steve goes inside the room with that person, Ravi looks inside from the outside of that room. Ravi sees a hot water pond inside the room that looked very old and a transparent ball was hanging on the top side of the ceiling, which was soaking the whole fog. Now Ravi was suspecting that person. Then Ravi runs to HR and Ravi slaps HR and runs out of the gym. Now HR is very angry, then he goes after Ravi and was about to start fighting with Ravi that Ravi speaks while stopping him = Wait HR, I had to do this because you were not listening to me.

HR = if I don't listen to you, will you beat me?

Ravi = No HR, you are not listening to me. Right now, you are under the control of that darkness which is controlling the mind of you and all those people who went to that gym.

HR = you have some misunderstanding. This is not possible.

Ravi = No, I have no misunderstanding because I saw a room in the gym which has a hot water pond.

Now before that Ravi ends his talk, then HR speaks in the middle = He is the room to rest. After exercising, everyone relaxes in hot water.

Now Ravi speaks angrily = Why don't you listen to me? I am saying that there is a transparent ball in the room that is hanging on the ceiling above and just now, I saw your boss going into that room. I think his life is in danger. Now you quickly transform into Rainbow Warrior and save your boss.

HR speaks with a sad face = so you could have said this without even a slap? You know how sad I felt that you slapped me in front of everyone.

Ravi = How long will you cry like children? You do not know that all of that is under the control of darkness, which means that they will not remember anything.

Now HR speaks happily = really?

Ravi = Yes. Now quickly turn into warrior and save the life of your boss

HR = OK.

## ~~ Lightning Of Fire Gives Me Power

## To End The Darkness ~~

# ~~ *Transform* ~~

**T**his Side = Steve's energy in that room was absorbed by the transparent ball that was hanging on the ceiling above. Now Mr. V and everyone from the gym were also in that room.

Mr. V who is actually Victor, he speaks = Mr. Steve is now going to exhaust all your energy. After which you will die.

Then the door of that room opens and a sound comes from that door = let them go right now. Because I know who you are Mr. V or may I call you Victor? One who works for Darkness and is spreading evil in this world.

Victor = you misunderstand.

Red warrior = I am not understanding anything wrong. Because I am Rainbow Red Warrior. To destroy evil forces. To drive away the darkness. To erase evil from evil people. I have brought the power of truth and goodness. Listen, if evil people want to escape, then leave the evil, otherwise you will end with that evil.

Victor = so you have recognized me. Boys it's time to Work out with that warrior.

The people who worked in the gym were already under control of Victor and now they attack the warrior to die.

The red warrior speaks while avoiding the attack = Wow how big they look to me. Like it's all hulk.

Here Victor collected a lot of people's Chi energy and while carrying that energy, he speaks to the warrior while leaving = Ok, so it is time for me to go, Rainbow warrior, but we will meet again. Hahaha...

Saying this, Victor leaves from there and the people of the gym, who Victor had controlled, all attack the warrior again. However, the red warrior escapes from them and thinks what to do now. Then the warrior realizes that his boss must be saved first. Therefore, he attacks that transparent ball [**Lightning of**

**Fire]** then that ball is destroyed.

Now the warrior sees that his boss was recovering from the destruction of that ball and he felt a lot of strength because that ball was absorbing the power of all the people in this room. Nevertheless, those gym people were still under control of Victor and attack the warrior again. Now the warrior does not avoid those controlled people, but fights them and by boxing the warrior easily injures those people.

Now the warrior thinks that these people do not have to die. Because he wants to eliminate evil and not those who have been controlled by evil. Then the warrior's eye falls on the head of those people because the headband of those people was shining very much. Now the warrior was thinking that these people might have been controlled through this headband.

Now the warrior attacks the headband of those people **[Lightning of Fire]** and the headband of those people is destroyed, which frees all the people of the gym from Victor's control.

Seeing this, the Red Warrior now departs from the place, calling that entire people goodbye.

**O**ther side here - Victor comes to Darkness with lots of Chi energy and speaks with Darkness = my boss, I have collected a lot of Chi energy from many people.

Darkness = very good, but what happened to that warrior?

Victor = my master, I will finish that warrior with my own hands now.

Darkness = No Victor, you will not be able to kill that warrior because that warrior has a lot of power. Even though he does not know how to use that power right now, still you will not be able to kill him so easily.

Victor = so my boss, how can we kill that warrior?

Darkness = a very simple answer to this, he is a warrior of light and we are demons of darkness. Now we just have to spread our darkness in the whole world so that people from all over the world will be under our control. Then that warrior will die easily. Hahaha......

<h1 style="text-align:center">(Chapter – 5)</h1>

The next day HR suddenly wakes up early in the morning after hearing the noise and going to his sister's room and he says that why are you making so much noise Harman? As soon as he says this, he sees that a cat was in his sister's room, so the cat runs away as soon as he opened the door of his sister's room.

Harman = this cat suddenly scared me.

HR = so you like cats so much?

Harman = Shut up, I don't like cats at all.

Then both hear their mother's voice and their mother says = you both started fighting in the morning? Stop fighting right now and quickly take a bath and get ready to eat food because breakfast is ready.

Both = Okay mother.

Now Harman goes to school after having dinner and HR goes to work after eating. On the way, HR gets Ravi and Ravi asks = HR, why your mood off today is?

HR = nothing. My little sister, she was just making noise in the morning and scared me.

Ravi = But why was she making noise?

HR = because she was scared when a cat came in her room.

Ravi = Oh, so your sister won't like cats?

HR = Yes, but she does not like any animals, maybe. Ok, so we meet later because I must go to work right now.

Ravi = Okay bye.

Other side here - Darkness = Victor, you now have another new plan so that we can spread evil increasingly in this world?

Victor = Yes, my boss, I have a very good plan, through this we can spread evil in the whole world and collect the chi energy of all people. This warrior will not be able to compete with us and we can easily kill those warriors.

Darkness = very good, but make this plan carefully because that warrior will come to stop you.

Victor = Yes, my boss, as you wish.

On this side, after Harman is discharged from school, when she comes out of school to go to her house, a puppy suddenly comes out in front of Harman and she is scared to see that puppy. At the same time, that puppy is also scared and runs away.

Now Harman's friend comes to her and asks her = Harman, why are you so afraid? he is just a small puppy.

Harman = Yes, but I do not like animals because in childhood a cat had bitten my finger and since then I do not like animals.

Friend = Oh no problem, I will take you to a new shop. Which is open today and we can buy the animal there and make it our pet.

Harman = I told you that I do not like animals, so why should I go there?

Friend = Yes but there is no real animal because it is a toy store and can only buy digital toys that look like animals.

Harman = wow, that would be a great shop. Let's go

Friend = Okay come on.

Now she goes to the shop with her friend before going home. When both arrived at that shop, Harman sees that there were many new toys in that shop which looks just like animals.

Now she goes to a toy looking like a dog. Then the shopkeeper comes to her and asks her = Do you like this toy?

Harman = yes but

Shopkeeper = But what, if you like it, you can take it.

Harman = But I have no money.

Shopkeeper = Never mind because today is the first day of the shop, we are giving this toy for free to the little ones and look carefully at this toy because the diamond is on the forehead of this toy. This diamond makes this toy look even more beautiful and the eyes of this toy, just look at its big eyes...

When the shopkeeper was saying this, she was looking into the eyes of this toy and the eyes of this toy start glowing. With which she is controlled by evil.

Now Harman and her friend and all the people came to buy toys at that shop. One by one evil was controlling them all.

**N**ow Harman and her friend go together towards home. While walking in the road, suddenly the same puppy comes in front of Harman, whom Herman was scared to see outside the school. Now Harman is not afraid to see that puppy because she was under control of evil and now evil was taking Chi energy from Harman through that toy. Due to this, the feeling of fear from Harman was over and all the other feelings were ending.

**N**ow when HR was coming home from work, Ravi meets HR again.

Ravi = Oh hey HR what happened, is something wrong?

HR = No, just wondering how to eliminate fear of my sister?

Ravi = Oh, then you take a cat to your sister and tell your sister that she should take that cat as her pet and it will eliminate her fear.

HR = Oh yes this is a good suggestion. Ok so let's meet tomorrow

Ravi = Okay but don't forget that you are also a warrior, so keep an eye on evil.

HR = OK Bye.

**N**ow HR takes a cat for his sister and comes home and then tells her sister = Hey Harman, will you make this cat your pet? Perhaps this will eliminate your fear.

However, she does not say anything, goes slowly to that cat, and kicks him, causing the cat to run away.

HR said angrily = what did you do?

She picks up the toy and speaks = Now this is my pet and I don't want any more animals.

As soon as she speaks, the mother calls them both to have dinner. Now when both sit down to eat dinner and their father says = Why do you both keep fighting?

HR = She was fighting with me because I was just trying to get over her fear.

Harman = No, I do not get over my fear because I have found a new animal, that does not scare me.

Father = really and which animal is that?

Harman shows that toy and says = this is that animal.

HR = But this is a toy that looks like a dog and this is not a real animal.

Father = Harvinder, do not break your sister's dreams because now she is small and she will grow up, then her fear will disappear.

HR = Well Okay.

When everyone has eaten, they all go to their respective rooms. Now Harman puts that toy on the table and sits in front of that toy, from which evil starts taking Harman's chi energy. She then watches that toy overnight.

The next day HR's mother says to him = HR, go and wake up your sister because she will be late for go to school.

Now HR comes knocking on the door of his sister's room = Harman wake up now because you will be late for school.

Harman = Today I want to stay at home.

HR speaks in shock = what?

Now HR slowly opens the door to his sister and sees that his sister was sitting on the chair and saying = Well, now both of us will always be together.

Seeing this, HR does not feel Harman's health well and he tells his mother that Harman's health is not well today and she will stay at home today. Now HR goes to work.

When HR arrives at his work, he sees that some of the girls in his office brought a toy resembling an animal, as he saw it with his sister.

HR speaks to Ajay = wow, this toy animal has become quite famous among girls.

Ajay = Yes, since this toy has come in the market, every girl does not want to see anyone else.

That's when their boss comes to the office and everyone tells those girls that the boss is coming and you hide your toys. Now the girl hides those toys. However, as soon as the boss says good morning, one girl is unable to live without seeing that toy and she takes all those toys out.

Boss = what is happening and why did all of you girls bring these toys to the office? Bring these toys to me and when you are discharged, take these toys from me.

As soon as Steve says this, he tries to get a toy from girl, and then this girl pushes him and says = Stay away from me because I will never take this toy away from my eyes. Now I am going home.

Saying this, all the other girls who have that toy also go away, telling them to go home.

Now Steve tells his employees = don't worry all of you because those girls may have brought the toy office by mistake. Everything will be fine by tomorrow. You all do your work.

Now after his boss goes to his room, HR asks Ajay = Hey Ajay, did you feel wrong in these toys?

Ajay = this toy is very beautiful in appearance and the diamond on his forehead was making these toys somewhat strange.

HR = Yes but when my sister caught the toy she was behaving strangely.

Ajay = so you should go and see that toy store.

HR = absolutely and will you go with me?

Ajay = Oh sorry because I have work at home today.

HR = Ok, so I will go on my own.

Ajay = Will you go alone?

HR = Yes because I care about my sister.

Ajay = very good, you are good brother.

HR = Thank you.

Now, after being discharged from work, HR reaches the toy store and as soon as he starts going inside that shop, he feels very strange. Like it is very evil inside. Then a voice is heard from behind him. Hey, Eye on Top.

Then HR speaks while turning back = that voice. ......

Now HR looks back and says = you again! Why do you come repeatedly in my life?

Rosella = I can say the same to you.

Now HR looks at her with anger and Rosella speaks to him = you are no longer a child and you are not going to buy toys for yourself? Is it true?

HR = Why?

Rosella = Just asking, because I had never seen an older child like the one you play with toys.

HR speaks angrily = shut up! –

Now HR goes inside the shop saying this to Rosella.

When he goes inside the shop then shopkeeper comes to the HR and he tells HR = Can I help you with something?

HR = No thanks, I will see for myself.

When HR sees those toys, He finds Ravi inside that shop, then HR tells Ravi = Ravi what are you doing at this place?

Ravi = I was feeling something wrong at this place and I came to know that by looking in the eyes of these toys, children start behaving strangely.

HR = Oh, so let me see what is in this toy's eye.

Now HR looks in the eye of this toy, then Ravi says = No HR, you don't look in its eyes...

However, it was too late and HR was looking into the eye of the toy that evil has controlled HR's mind. Now the shopkeeper comes to HR and asks = you can want to buy this toy.

HR = Yes.

Now HR comes out of the shop with that toy and starts going to his house and then Ravi stops HR and says, "Hey HR, where are you going with this toy?"

HR = you stay away from me because I don't like you.

Speaking of this, HR starts going through a street where a small child falls down playing alone and starts crying. However, HR ignores the child and leaves the street. Here Ravi chases HR and sees that HR did not raise the child after that child falls.

Now Ravi picks up that child and laughs. After that Ravi went to HR, forced the toy away from HR, and threw it away. As a result, the diamond on the head of the toy breaks and the HR becomes conscious.

Ravi = Oh thank goodness you have recovered.

HR = Oh, Hey Ravi what happened to me?

Ravi = When you looked in the eyes of that toy, then the diamond in the head of that toy was shining, due to which you started to act strange.

HR = Oh yes, I remembered when I saw that toy; I was so scared that I could not control my mind and now this toy should be removed from my sister.

Speaking of this, HR runs towards his house and Ravi follows him.

When HR reaches home, he tries to get that toy from his sister, but his sister does not give him that toy, because his sister was completely possessed by evil. Now Harman pushes her brother vigorously and runs away from the house with that toy.

Now HR gets depressed and sits in the chair and asks Ravi = Ravi, what should I do now?

Ravi = this is not the time to be sad because now you must go to that toy store and end the evil.

HR = Correct, but if I saw those toy eyes again, I would be scared again.

Ravi = HR, Stop being afraid because you are the Red Rainbow Warrior and think of your sister. Now let's quickly turn you into warrior and put an end to that evil.

HR = OK.

## ~~ Lightning Of Fire Gives Me Power
## To End The Darkness ~~

# ~~ *Transform* ~~

**O**ther Side there, a lot of people came to that toy shop which have been controlled by evil and most of them have children.

Now the shopkeeper who is actually a demon, orders all these people to spread these toys among their people.

When the demon said this, the door of the shop suddenly opens and a sound comes from this door = Your game is over now.

Demon = Who are you?

Red Warrior = I am Rainbow Red Warrior. To destroy evil forces. To drive away the darkness. To erase evil from evil people. I have brought the power of truth and goodness. Listen, if evil people want to escape, then leave the evil, otherwise you will end with that evil. Because I have come to end this evil game.

Demon = So you have come Rainbow Warrior.

By speaking this the demon turns into a monster which is its true form and everybody also turns into a monster.

Red warrior speaks fearfully like children = this is so scary.

Then the demon and everyone attack the Red Warrior. Now the warrior runs away from this demon and thinks = what should I do now?

Now the warrior, seeing this, thinks that all those people have held those toys till now, but why?

Then suddenly the warrior realizes that the demon must have controlled the people with these toys.

Now the warrior thinks that if all these toys are broken, will all these people be free from the control of the demon?

Then suddenly the warrior remembers that when the monster is controlled by the people, then the diamond in the forehead of these toys starts glowing, so now I must destroy the diamond in the forehead of all these toys. Only then will these people be free from demon possession. Maybe?

Now the Red Warrior attacks with his power **[Lightning of Fire]** and the diamond of the head of all these toys is destroyed and all these people are freed from the control of that demon.

Now the demon comes to attack the warrior and speaks angrily = You have destroyed all my plan and I will not leave you alive now.

Here the warrior runs out of the shop to escape from that demon, but that demon captures the warrior with his power, then Ravi's voice comes from someplace and Ravi says = Red warrior you will see that this demon's neck is shining behind, attack there because it is weak point of demon and it will destroy the demon.

Then the Red Warrior strikes the back of this demon's neck with his power **[Lightning of Fire]** and at the same time the demon is finished.

Now after defeating the demon, the Red Warrior speaks to himself = Oh, this demon is becoming stronger. Now it is getting difficult to defeat these demons and this time Mysterious Girl did not come to save me.

When all this red warrior was speaking by himself, Harman comes running out of the shop and says to the red warrior = Hello sir, thank you for saving us from that demon.

Red warrior = Never mind, it was my duty.

Harman = But what is your name?

Red Warrior = My name is Red Rainbow Warrior.

Harman = wow, you are a superhero?

Red Warrior = Yes, I am.

Harman = wow, thank you again and you fought those demons with great bravery.

Red warrior = he was nothing. That demon was making all your fear his power. Because fear is the only thing we should never fear. Do you fear anyone?

Harman = Yes, actually I am afraid of animals.

Red warrior = Oh, then you should try to befriend a small animal which will end your fear and then you will not be afraid of any big animal.

Harman = You say anything. I will try with a small animal.

Red warrior = very good. So now I must go.

Harman = Can I see you again?
Red Warrior = Yes, of course, see you later.
Harman = Goodnight, Red Rainbow Warrior.
Saying this, the Red Warrior goes on his way.

**O**n the other side Ravi is hiding and watching everything.
Now Ravi speaks with a red warrior at some other place = So you did it very well that your sister's fear of animals came out of her mind. Now the demon this time was more powerful than before. Therefore, you should be more alert than before.

Red Warrior = Yes, you are right. So now we meet tomorrow. good night.

Ravi = Okay, see you tomorrow.

**N**ext day - Today Harman brings a puppy into the house and her mother is shocked to see this and speaks = HR, was this your suggestion.

HR = No, but it's good that She is not afraid of animals anymore.

Mother = Yes, but for how long?........

# (Chapter – 6)

**H**ere, painful music was playing at the dark place. Victor stood in a panic in front of Darkness.

Darkness = Victor, for a few days, that warrior is looking weak and that warrior knows our demons is very hard to beat.

Victor = Yes, my boss.

Darkness = Now the time has come that we should bring our evil in every human's house quickly.

Victor = Yes, my boss. But how?

Darkness = you listening to this music?

Victor = Yes.

Darkness = So take this CD of this music and play it in some place where every person can hear it. In this way, we can control a lot of humans with this music.

Victor = As you wish my boss. This is a very good plan.

Now speaking this, Victor gives this CD to one of his demon girl and asks her to play his music along with the music of humans.

**O**ther side here – HR was listening to music during his free time at work, then Ajay comes to him and asks = Hey HR what are you listening to?

HR = I am listening to Baarish Yaariyan music.

Ajay = wow, this music is very romantic.

HR = Yes, but I do not know who is the singer?

Ajay = Do you not know the name of the singer of this song?

HR = Yes, but why?

Ajay = Singer of this song is Mohammed Irfan and wrote this song for his girlfriend.

HR = Oh how lucky is that girl.

Ajay = Yes and you know that Mohammed Irfan has now come to our city recording studio to record his new song.

HR = Really, can we go to meet him today?

Ajay = Okay, today we go to meet him in the studio after work, but don't let the security guard of that studio meet Mohammed Irfan.

HR = Never mind, but we should still go.

Ajay = Okay.

It is raining in the evening. Outside the studio, a girl standing speaks to herself = Today I must express my love.

At the same time, that demon girl goes to the recording room in the studio because there was no human in that room right now. Now that demon girl speaks to herself while putting that diabolical CD in the recording player = Now I must put the virus of evil in every music of this human with this CD so that the evil will get the humans in control quickly.

Now this demon girl had inserted this CD in the player that suddenly the door of the recording room opens and that demon girl quickly hides.

From that door, that singer Mohammed Irfan comes into the room and speaks to himself = Oho, I am so careless. I forgot this CD at this place.

When Mohammed Irfan was speaking, the demon girl saw that Mohammed Irfan had accidentally picked up her CD.

Now that demon girl was going to die Mohammed Irfan to get that CD when suddenly the security guard speaks from outside the recording room door = Mohammed Irfan sir, a girl has come to meet you in the lobby below and we know that Right now you do not want to meet your fan, but when that girl showed your personal visiting card, we understood that she will be your special friend.

Mohammed Irfan = Okay, so let's go to meet that girl.

Now Mohammed Irfan takes that CD with him to the studio lobby to meet the girl and the demon girl chases Mohammed

Irfan.

Now Mohammed Irfan comes into the lobby and looks at the girl and speaks = Why have you come to meet me in the rain at this time and you have not even taken an umbrella. Now all your clothes are wet.

That girl = I came to wish you a happy birthday because tomorrow is your birthday.

Mohammed Irfan = Hey, you could have told me this on the phone.

That girl = yes but…

Mohammed Irfan = No problem. Look, I have recorded a new song and I wanted to talk to you about the title of this song because you had helped me to give music in this song.

As soon as Mohammed Irfan says this, his assistant comes to him and says = Sir, it's time for your next song.

Mohammed Irfan = What, so soon? And you forgive me, you take this CD and tell me whether this music is recorded well or not and now you should go to your music club.

That girl = yes, we will meet later.

Mohammed Irfan = Okay and I tell the security guard to give you an umbrella so that you don't get wet.

Mohammed Irfan, goes on recording by speaking it and then the girl speaks to herself = Today again I could not express my love.

Here the demon girl secretly looks at Mohammed Irfan and that girl and she realizes that Mohammed Irfan has given that CD to that girl.

On the other side HR and Ajay are discharged from work and see that it is raining very fast today.

HR = Oh it seems we won't be able to meet Mohammed Irfan today.

Ajay = Probably yes.

HR = Okay Ajay, we meet again at work tomorrow.

Ajay = Okay good night.

Now Ajay goes to his house and HR thinks of staying at Ritu's cafe on his way home. When HR reaches Ritu's café, as soon as he starts going inside, suddenly a girl comes running and collides with HR, which causes both of them to fall and both of them get dirty.

Now HR clothes were dirty so he speaks angrily to that girl = Hey, what have you done, all my clothes have become dirty. I will not leave you now

This girl was very scared before and as soon as HR spoke this girl became even more scared. Then fearfully said = Don't kill me - please don't kill me.

HR = Wait, I'm not going to kill you. I just said it in anger.

This girl = Thank you and let's talk on the go?

HR = OK. Now tell me why you were running

This girl = you will not listen to me. But someone was targeting me.

HR = what, who?

This girl = monster.

HR = What, monster?

This girl = hmmm

HR = Okay, now tell me the whole story from the beginning.

This girl = Okay, when I was going to my work, I was going through a street to take a short way, then I saw a girl in that street, so I tried to talk to that girl but that girl had someone Did not reply and when I started going to that girl, that girl turned into a monster and I was very scared, then I started running away from that place and bump into you while running. So, all this happened...... I know all this may have been my imagination but it all seemed real...... Oh, I'm sorry, maybe I bored you by hearing this stupid story.

HR = No, nothing like that and maybe you are right. However, what is your job?

This girl = oh, my job, I'm a musician and my job are to play music in the night music club.

HR = wow, that would be a great job.

This girl = Yes and right now I must go to my work otherwise I will be delayed from going to my work and sorry again for your clothes.

HR = Oh no problem and can we meet again?

This girl = yes absolutely, good night.

Now that girl goes to her job but HR speaks to himself while thinking about that monster = can this girl who was speaking be true?

As HR says this, a voice comes from behind him = Yes HR it can be true.

Then HR turns around and sees Ravi there. Now HR asks Ravi = when did you come?

Ravi = I was following you for quite a while.

HR said shockingly = What, when will you stop chasing me like this?

Ravi = It is my job because I have been sent to watch over all the warriors.

HR = You stop chasing because now we are friends.

Ravi = Yes, it is.

HR = Ok, so now you tell me what you were saying about that monster?

Ravi = I told you earlier that, evil is trying to take possession of this earth, but that evil is not so powerful, so that evil is not able to take possession of this earth at once. That is why evil is slowly controlling the minds of all the people, and perhaps this girl was also tried to control by some evil demon.

HR = What should we do now?

Ravi = I think we should chase that girl.

HR = You are talking about chasing again.

Ravi = Hey, you are my friend but she is not and besides that we must find out if that demon girl comes again to this girl or not.

HR = Yes, but hold on. I change my disguise.

Ravi = Okay.

HR = OK, **"Power Hidden"**. Now look, this disguise is correct.

Ravi = Yes, let's go now?

HR = Yes, okay let's go.

Now both go inside the music club.

Here when that demon girl is unable to catch the girl, she talks to Victor with her power = Sir, the CD is lost from me.

Victor said in surprise = What, you foolish. how did this happen?

Demon Girl = Sir, as you said, I started that CD in the recording company to put that virus in the music of humans, but a person suddenly came to that place and that person took that CD.

Victor = You stop giving me excuses and that person should have been killed at the same time.

Demon Girl = forgive me

Victor = Anyway, now you must take that CD back and if anyone comes in your way, then you finish it. Do you understand?

Demon Girl = yes sir.

Victor = Now if you are not able to conceive this plan then you will have to lose your life. Got it

Demon Girl = yes sir.

Saying this, Victor breaks his contact and the demon girl goes to get the CD from that girl.

Other side here - when HR and Ravi come inside the music club, Ravi says = O HR, we should sit at some side place so that the girl cannot see us.

HR = Yes Okay.

When both of them sit on the side seat, the servant of that club comes to them and that servant asks them = Sir, would you like to take anything?

First Ravi was going to say that HR said before that = What are the things for free?

Ravi and that servant were shocked to hear this and Ravi said to that servant = sorry it was just joking.

HR understood and said again = Sorry, excuse me, you do this by adding milk in a glass and bring in its chocolate?

Now hearing this Ravi and that servant are shocked again and now Ravi angrily speaks softly to HR = O HR, has your lottery come out that you are asking for things for free and it is your house that gives you get a free chocolate milk shake? at this place, High class people smoke cigarettes and alcohol.

Now HR understood the right thing and said to that servant = Forgive me because I was still joking and we don't want anything right now.

Hearing this, that servant leaves the place.

Now that girl starts playing music from the violin and HR speaks after listening to her music = wow, what a beautiful music this girl plays.

When that girl leaves the place playing this music, Ravi sees that HR fell asleep while listening to music and then Ravi speaks awake to HR = Hey HR why did you sleep? Quickly get up and see, the girl has gone towards the basement parking of this club.

**H**ere when this girl reaches the parking of the basement of this club, the servant of the basement of this club speaks to this girl = Madam, I have turned your car on.

This girl = Thank you, you can go now.

When that servant leaves from the basement parking, this girl holds the CD in her hand and speaks to herself = How should I express my love?

This girl had just said that a black smoke started coming in front of this girl and from that smoke came out the same girl who had seen this girl in the street before and now this girl was so scared to see that girl in front of her and It screamed loudly.

Here HR and Ravi were coming from the staircase in the basement parking, then both of them heard this voice and HR said = It seems to be that same girl's voice.

Ravi = Yes, maybe She is in danger.

Then both quickly reach the parking lot and HR sees the girl fall on the ground and go to gets up and asks the girl = Hey how did you fall on the ground?

So, this girl sees that she does not have that CD and speaks = Do not ask anything right now because I must chase someone right now.

Hearing this, HR and Ravi also speak that we will also go with you.

This girl = Okay then hurry sit in the car.

**N**ow this girl drives the car very fast and HR is scared to see her driving and says = Hey just drive slowly because I am scared.

This girl = No, I must stop that monster from carrying that CD.

Ravi and HR both speak together = What, a CD?

That girl = Yes and you are the same guy I met a while back.

HR says in his mind that hey I have come in my real form and Ravi speaks softly in HR's ear = Hey HR, when you were coming from the stairs to the basement parking, you changed into your true form Had gone.

HR = Oh....

Now HR speaks to this girl = Yes, I am the same boy and you were very afraid of that monster earlier, so now you are not afraid, why?

This girl = Yes, because I do not want anyone to take that CD from me.

HR = But what is so special in that CD?

This girl = that CD was given to me by Mohammed Irfan.

HR & Ravi = Mohammed Irfan?

This girl = Yes, because I give music in Mohammed Irfan's songs.

HR = Oh, then you are not afraid anymore because love kills all fear.

This girl speaks blushing = No, I just give music in Mohammed Irfan's songs.

HR = No need to shame you, if you love then say it and anyway, I saw Mohammed Irfan's name on the CD case in that parking lot.

This girl said with surprise = What, then why have you both come with me?

HR = We have come to support love and we do not want another person to take the sign of love of a loved one.

This girl = Oh, I get it.

Ravi = Okay, then tell me one thing, when that demon girl took that CD from you, then why did she not kill you?

HR = Ravi, how are you talking, are you not happy to see her alive?

This girl = Because when that demon girl took the CD from me, she was saying that she has delayed her work and she does not want to waste her time in dying me and then she left the place quickly.

HR = Oh, so now I see which way she went.

Now HR sees something flying above and HR looks at him and speaks = there in the sky. What, that is a Gargoyle?

Ravi = where?

This girl = Yes, this is the same monster girl who took my CD.

HR = how is that?

This girl = When that monster girl came to take the CD from me, she turned into a Gargoyle.

Ravi = Yes, I can see her because now that the rain has stopped, the Gargoyle is clearly visible.

This girl = Ok, so now tell me where did that monster girl go?

HR = She is going over the building of that recording station.

Now quickly this girl stops the car outside the recording station and when everyone gets off this car, so this girl speaks = Oh God, Mohammed Irfan and his staff are still recording in this recording station.

Hearing this, both HR and Ravi are shocked and speak together = What?

Here when that demon girl comes to the recording room, she says with a smile = Now I have got this CD and now I will be able to complete this plan because when I went to get this CD, I put you all to sleep and Now I will change the mind of all of you with this CD so that you will all accept my rule. Hahaha......

When this demon girl was about to put that CD in the player to play, HR, Ravi and that girl suddenly open the recording room door and Ravi pushes the demon girl and the CD falls from her hand and HR takes that CD in his hand and says = Stop all this now.

Demon Girl = You will not be able to stop my plan.

Speaking of this, the demon girl turns into Gargoyle and HR

starts to get scared.

Gargoyle = Give me that CD

HR speaks fearfully = Which CD?

This girl = Hey, you have caught my CD.

HR said fearfully = what?

Ravi = HR in your hand.

HR asks fearfully = in whose hands?

Gargoyle = Enough, give me that CD.

Saying this, Gargoyle attacks HR and HR collapses.

Ravi = HR, are you, all right?

Now Gargoyle grabs this girl and speaks to HR = If you want to see this girl alive then give me that CD.

This girl = you don't worry me and don't give it to this CD.

Here Mohammed Irfan wakes up from sleep and sees that his friend is in trouble and he quickly pushes the Gargoyle from behind which saves the girl but he gets hurt.

Now Ravi speaks to HR = HR we should go to some empty place or else all these people will die.

HR = Okay come on.

As soon as he says this, HR speaks to Gargoyle by showing this CD = O Demon, do you want this CD, then follow me.

When both Ravi and HR leave from that place, both of them go towards the concert hall and while leaving, Ravi speaks to HR = O HR quickly turn you into a Red Warrior.

HR = OK

## ~~ Lightning Of Fire Gives Me Power
## To End The Darkness ~~

## ~~ *Transform* ~~

Here the demon girl sees HR transforming into a red warrior.

On reaching the concert hall, Ravi tells Red warrior = Red warrior, I hide somewhere and now you finish this demon girl, okay.

Now the Red Warrior breaks that CD and speaks to that demon

girl = O Gargoyle, now this CD is broken so you surrender now, because I am Rainbow Red Warrior. To destroy evil forces. To drive away the darkness. To erase evil from evil people. I have brought the power of truth and goodness. Listen, if evil people want to escape, then leave the evil, otherwise you will end with that evil.

Ravi speaks surprised = O Red warrior, is it important to always speak this line of yours?

Gargoyle = Never mind because I know who you are. So, when I kill you and I tell this to my boss, so my boss will forgive me for breaking that CD and my boss will reward me for also killing you.

Now the Red Warrior thinks in his mind = Oh now this demon girl must be finished or else my family and all my friends will be in danger.

Right now, the Red Warrior was thinking that the demon girl suddenly attacks with strong sound waves and the Red Warrior falls on the stage of the concert hall.

When the Red Warrior falls on the stage of the concert hall, he thinks in his mind that this demon girl is stronger than all the demons whom I had fought before. what do I do now? Suddenly Red Warrior sees a microphone on the stage and he gets an idea.

Now when Gargoyle strikes again, the Red Warrior throws the microphone in front of the attack of that Gargoyle's sound wave, which breaks that microphone and the sound wave from the concert hall speakers in a terrible way Goes back and collides with that Gargoyle.

Causing Gargoyle to be greatly injured.

Ravi = Red warrior You have a chance to defeat that demon girl. Attack now

Red warrior = I get it. **[Lightning of Fire]**

Now this attack goes to the demon girl and the demon girl is destroyed at the same time.

When the demon girl is finished, then both go to see Mohammed Irfan and that girl.

Now both of them hide from outside the recording room and see that Mohammed Irfan, this girl and the rest of the staff are now safe.

Now the Red Warrior turns back to HR and starts going home with Ravi. On the go, HR tells Ravi = finally that girl can say the feelings of her heart and now Mohammed Irfan will marry that girl or not.

Ravi = You are right, but now you will have to work harder in your powers because these demons of Victor are becoming more powerful.

HR = Okay and you saw this time, the Mysterious Girl did not come.

Ravi = Yes, but you should not wait for that girl.

HR = Yes, but i like her.

Ravi = What?

HR = I mean, I like her coming.

Ravi = Oh.......

HR = Okay so now my house has come and now we meet tomorrow.

Ravi = Okay good night.

HR = Good night.

(Chapter – 7)

The next day HR goes towards his work and speaks to himself = Oh no, today my bike has a problem, otherwise I would have reached work early today. Don't know on which day I will arrive at my work early?

Shortly after HR arrives at work, Ajay comes to HR and says = Hey HR you know today a dance competition is happening in our city and the first prize in that competition is Rs 50,000 / -.

That is when Neha speaks from behind = You both came to know about this competition. By the way, I was coming to tell both of you about this competition and Shilpa Shetty has come to choose the winner.

HR = What, Bollywood Star Shilpa Shetty. wow, that would be awesome.

Ajay = So now I am going to participate in this competition.

Neha = You take participate it but only one winner of this competition.

Ajay = who?

Neha speaks by pointing to HR = this.

HR = Me? Am i really a winner? wow........

Other side here - Darkness scolds Victor = Victor, after you losing that CD have spoiled all our plans and the demon girl you sent knew the true form of that warrior, but before telling us She was already destroyed. What will you do now Victor because that warrior is slowly becoming powerful?

Victor speaks fearfully = My boss you don't worry because I have just come to know that there is a dance competition in the city and there will be a lot of people together. Now we can spread evil in people by taking advantage of that competition.

Darkness = Okay then i see and this time nothing should go wrong.

Victor = As you wish my boss.

**H**ere Ajay and HR take early leave from work and come to practice at HR's house to participate in dance competition.

HR = Hey Ajay how will we practice?

Ajay = You do not worry because I have brought some CDs of songs and you keep doing as I say. Okay.

HR = OK.

Now both start dance practice. However, HR does not do as Ajay says and HR repeatedly collides with Ajay while dancing, so Ajay gets angry and speaks the wrong word to HR and HR also starts speaking the wrong word to Ajay.

Saying this, Ajay leaves HR's house. Now Harman comes to HR's room and asks HR = Why were you fighting with your friend?

HR speaks in crying face = He is no longer my friend because I am not able to dance with him.

Harman = So what, if you can't dance with it, maybe you should dance with someone else and it should be your friend.

Now HR speaks happily = you are right.

Harman = What.

HR = Whatever you said is correct.

Harman = Both of you should be friends.

HR = No.

Harman = What.

HR = Never mind. Now you should leave my room.

Now, by taking Harman out of his room, HR closes the door.

Then Harman speaks to herself = Don't know what will happen to it because sometimes it is happy and suddenly it starts crying and suddenly starts getting angry.

Now HR calls Ravi and says = O Ravi, come to my house and meet me right now.

**H**ere Ajay goes to his house and calls Neha and asks Neha to come to his house.

When Neha comes to Ajay's house, Ajay tells Neha = Hey Neha, we should participate in a dance competition together and both of us will dance on pop song and for this you should wear this boys' outfits.

Neha = Oh that is good.

Now Neha wears these clothes and asks Ajay = How do I look?

Ajay = You are looking good and now no one can stop us from winning this competition.

Neha = Thank you.

And here, when Ravi reaches HR's house, HR also prepares Ravi to dance with him.

**O**ther side at night - when Shilpa Shetty sits on her bed to sleep, suddenly the other demon girl of Victor comes into its room with magic. So Shilpa is scared to see the demon girl and shouts loudly because the demon girl was in her true form. Then the demon girl quickly faints Shilpa and then changes into its form.

Just then, the security guard knocks Shilpa's room on hearing Shilpa's scream.

The demon girl asks the security guard as Shilpa = what happened?

Security Guard = Madam, when I heard the sound of chilling, I came to see that everything is fine.

The demon girl speaks as Shilpa = Yes, all right, I was watching the movie, then there was noise coming from the TV.

Security Guard = Okay Madam. good night.

Demon Girl as Shilpa = Goodnight.

**T**he next day the demon girl makes this announcement as Shilpa = Now two winners will be chosen in this competition, so anyone can participate in this competition.

Here some people talk on HR work while talking to each other that from now on, two winners will be selected in this dance competition and everyone is participating in it.

When all these were speaking, Ajay and HR were listening to these people and both of them look at each other and say in their mind = I have found my partner, what will happen to you now.

Now many people from HR work take early leave from work to participate in that competition and HR was going to participate in that competition with Ravi. So, Ravi stops on the way and says = Hey HR I cannot participate in this competition.

HR = Oh are you afraid of dancing on stage?

Ravi = No, I am afraid that if you become famous then what will happen to our mission and then that evil will end this world, along with your family and your friends.

Now HR makes a face like crying.

Ravi = Your cry will not change my answer.

HR speaks with a crying face = I have no friend.

Speaking of this, HR runs away from Ravi.

Now running, HR sees Rosella in front of him and then HR walks into a quiet street, then stops in that street and thinks in his mind that Rosella has not seen him.

But Rosella sees HR, then goes to HR and says = Hey Eye on Top what are you doing here and why are you crying like children?

But HR does not reply.

Rosella = I think you have not been selected in the competition whose people are talking about these days.

Now HR speaks angrily = Hey listen Rosella I don't want to talk to you, okay.

Saying this HR goes to his house and speaks his mind while leaving = Oh, this girl always makes me angry.

And here the other side - the dance competition was happening in the cricket field and all the people who came to participate in this dance competition are selected.

The next day when HR arrives at work. So, while opening the door of office, he speaks to himself = I am late again and do not know what the boss will say today.

But as soon as HR opens the door of the office, HR sees that all the office staff is practicing the competition and when HR meets the boss in boss's room, then he sees that the boss is also behaving strangely while practicing that competition.

Now HR meets Ravi after being discharged from work.

Ravi = Are you not angry with me that I did not let you participate in that competition?

HR = No, but I am happy because my office staff is behaving strangely about that competition.

Ravi = Oh so maybe this is the next step of evil?

HR = I was suspicious after seeing this strange behavior.

Ravi = I am glad that you are taking care of this work.

HR = Okay so tomorrow we go to the practice place of this competition and see what is happening.

Ravi = Okay.

The next day when HR and Ravi reach the competition. So, HR says = Oh this place is very big. But this is strange because this place was never used, so why now?

Here the other side was telling the demon girl to all the people = Practice all of you together because to reach the last stage, you all should have a lot of power.

Here HR and Ravi hiding sees these people.

HR = Hey Ravi, watch all these people dancing together because they are doing strange movements while dancing.

Ravi = Yes you are right.

HR = Ravi look there, is that Shilpa Shetty and the crystal ball with him is pulling some waves coming from all the people.

Ravi = It cannot be real Shilpa Shetty because it is of waves of energy.

Right now, Ravi was saying that the demon girl listens to the voice of both of them and asks both of them in their real form = May I help you?

Here Ravi is shocked to see its true form and HR is scared to see its true form and runs away and hides in the bathroom.

Then Ravi goes to the bathroom behind HR and tells HR from the outside of the bathroom = O HR now is the time you should turn into a rainbow warrior and save these people by destroying this monster.

HR = But I'm scared.

Ravi = This is not the time to be afraid because if you do not save them, no one else will come to save them.

Now HR comes out of the bathroom and says = Ok I will try.

## ~~ Lightning Of Fire Gives Me Power To End The Darkness ~~

## ~~ *Transform* ~~

**H**ere everyone faints while dancing and the demon girl says to herself = Now I have got all of you Chi energy.

Then a man on the stage says to the demon girl = Now it is time for you to finish this dance competition and give all these people their energy.

Demon Girl = Why, who are you?

Now the light falls on the stage and then the Red Warrior speaks in that light = I am Rainbow Red Warrior. To destroy evil forces. To drive away the darkness. To erase evil from evil people. I have brought the power of truth and goodness. Listen, if evil people want to escape, then leave the evil, otherwise you will end with that evil.

Now the demon girl returns to her true form.

Red warrior = You can't scare me anymore.

As soon as the Red Warrior says this, the demon girl attacks him and the Red Warrior hides in the stadium chairs, avoiding that attack.

Demon girl = You cannot hide from me.

This side Red Warrior speaks to himself = I must overcome my fear and destroy this demon girl.

Speaking of this, the red warrior comes out of the chairs and sees where the demon girl is, when the demon girl speaks in the air = Are you looking for me?

The demon girl suddenly attacks by saying this and the red

warrior begins to be imprisoned in a crystal, then suddenly a light beam that looks like a rose comes from the other side and collides with that crystal and the red the warrior is freed from that crystal.

Demon Girl = what's happening? Who is there?

Red Warrior = Mysterious Girl.

Mysterious Girl = You should overcome your fears Red Warrior.

Red Warrior = Thank you Mysterious Girl.

Mysterious Girl = Never mind. I got to go now.

Demon girl = You cannot run away after spoiling my plan.

Saying this, the demon girl starts following the Mysterious Girl, then the Red Warrior thinks that it is time to destroy this demon and the Red Warrior strikes **[Lightning of Fire]**

But the Red Warrior's attack is reflected by that demon girl and comes back.

Now the Red Warrior bends down to avoid this attack, and then this attack goes to collides with the crystal ball that destroys the crystal ball, and the Red Warrior sees that the demon girl is also being destroyed.

Now the red warrior meets Ravi and tells Ravi = O Ravi this time Mysterious Girl came to save me.

Ravi = Yes, I saw and this time you had a lucky time because your attack accidentally hit the crystal ball and destroyed that demon girl.

**H**ere, everyone was awake because they were getting their energy back, but no one remembered much more.

Now on the other side, the real Shilpa Shetty wakes up in her room and sees that she was sleeping for a few days, but why she didn't remember anything and speaks to herself = I think I am working too much, so I should take leave for a few days.

**H**ere, when Ravi say HR to goodbye and goes on his way, Ravi gets a call from someone and he telling Ravi on the phone = You will find the next warrior tomorrow and evil will send his demon to die the red warrior because maybe the red warrior Human form is evil known.

Ravi speaks surprised = what?

**"Who's the next Warrior and How to evil know HR true form?"**

# (Chapter – 8)

Here, Darkness speaks to Victor = Victor this time also your demon has destroyed in the hands of that warrior.

Victor = You don't worry my boss because I have a new plan.

Darkness = Oh what should I do for you because even this plan will probably fail, but still tell me what plan you have?

Victor = My boss, this time I have told my demon to control all the people in a computer class and it will not make much noise. In this way, we can take the Chi energy of all people silently, so that we will become stronger. After this, we can finish that warrior easily.

Darkness = Okay then start this plan.

Victor = As you wish my boss.

Here HR's house, HR was awake till late night watching TV, when HR's father tells him to sleep.

HR = Oh dad, I'm not sleepy right now.

Father = Harvinder Today I have called your boss to give you a high post in which you will have to run a computer, so you should sleep now to go to work early tomorrow.

Now HR speaks sadly = Oh Dad, okay.

The next day Ravi comes to HR early in the morning and speaks while going to HR work with HR = Hey HR I have a new news for you.

HR = Wait Ravi I also have a new news for you.

Ravi = I will tell first. I have received news that a spy of evil will come to you to die at your work and now you must find out who he is.

HR = Oh really and you know that my dad told the boss that now I should work on the computer.

Ravi = This is very good.

HR = No it's not good because I don't know how to run a computer properly.

Ravi = Oh.

HR = Okay, so we meet later because my place of work has come.

Ravi = Okay but keep an eye on that spy.

HR = OK.

Now Ajay comes to HR and speaks to HR = Hey HR now you will work on computer, am I right?

HR = Yes and you are not angry with me?

Ajay = No, why did you think so?

HR = No, nothing.

Ajay = HR, you know today a new girl is start working in our office and that girl will work with you on the computer.

HR speaks in mind = is she the same spy girl whom Ravi told about.

As soon as HR thinks this in the mind, then suddenly Neha comes from behind and says = Hey boys, what are you doing?

That's why Ajay and HR get nervous and HR speaks = Neha, don't be scared like that.

Neha = Oh HR, when will you stop being afraid?

HR = I'm not afraid and what do you know about that girl, Neha?

Neha = Oh that girl. Her name is Ritika and she is a computer master.

HR and Ajay = what computer master.

Neha = I mean she knows all about computers.

Ajay = Oh no problem, I try to talk to that girl.

HR = Wait Ajay, you should not talk to that girl because I feel something strange.

Ajay = Why, do you want to talk to that girl first?

HR = There is no such thing.

Neha = Yes, there is no such thing because HR only talks to me.

HR = This is also incorrect.

Neha now said sadly = Oh no.

Ajay = O she is looking here.

Then HR laughs loudly and says = Oh Neha you also joke a lot. Hahaha....

Then Ajay and Neha also start laughing. Ha-Ha...

**N**ow after some time HR speaks to himself while walking in the road = Oh Dad, what was the need to tell the boss that I should work on the computer. Now the boss has quickly discharged me from work and said go to computer class to get more information about computer. OH... ☹

Now on the go, HR sees that new girl and HR thinks in his mind = maybe this girl is going to the computer class, where I am going. So, is this the same demon spy? I think Ravi must have got some wrong information because it has not done anything wrong to me yet. Maybe I should try talking to it.

Now HR calls that girl = Hey Ritika.

Ritika speaks looking at HR = Oh hey, you are HR.

HR = You said it right but how do you know my name?

Ritika = Neha told me at work and she also say that she like you and you get scared very quickly like children.

HR speaks with a smile = Oh no, she was just joking.

Ritika = Tell me more about yourself?

Now HR and Ritika talk on the way.

HR = I like watching TV, having fun and more.

Ritika = Oh don't you learn something else? Like a computer.

HR = No.

Ritika speaks slowly = But I like to learn.

HR = what? Learning, but what will you do after learning all this, are you from another planet? How weird.

Ritika = Am I weird?

Then HR suddenly stops and says = No, it was just a joke and let me introduce you to my friend. She runs this café.

Ritika = Okay.

**N**ow HR and Ritika go inside the café and Ritu looks at HR and says = Hey HR, how are you and who is this girl?
HR = Hey Ritu, this is my new friend Ritika.
Ritu = Oh hey Ritika, will you drink coffee?
Ritika = Okay.
HR = Okay, then we sit at this place for a while and Ritika, what is it in your backpack?
Ritika = This is my relative's laptop.
HR = Oh, So Does It Have Games?
Now Ritika speaks by turning on the laptop = yes it has games.
Now Ritika runs that game and HR is surprised to see this = wow, how fast you play this game.
Then suddenly Ritika remembers that she is late for computer class. Now it quickly starts leaving this place by putting its laptop in the backpack. Then HR says stopping it = Hey Ritika, where are you going so fast?
Ritika = our computer class.
HR = Oh well, see you later.
Ritika = Ok Bye.
After Ritika leaves, Ritu comes to HR and speaks = Hey HR, where did Ritika go?
HR = She has gone to her computer class.
Ritu = Oh so will you give this to Ritika.
HR = what is it?
Ritu = this is her pen-drive, maybe she forgot it.
Now HR speaks with a fake smile = Ok I will give it to her.

**H**ere when Ritika reaches computer class, she sees that she does not have her pen-drive, so she speaks to herself = Oh my pen-drive, maybe I forgot that pen-drive in the cafe.
Then suddenly Ritika's computer Sir comes to her and speaks = Hello Ritika, will you do my one thing.
Ritika speaks in a panic = Yes Sir.
Ritika's computer sir = will you watch this class for a while?

Ritika = Okay sir.

Ritika's computer sir = Okay then i will come now.

Ritika = Thank God, Sir did not ask about the pen-drive.

**N**ow HR reaches outside the building of this computer class and seeing this building, he says = Oh, I do not want to go to this class.

As soon as HR says this, a sudden sound comes from behind = Hey Eye on Top, you are looking top again and what are you talking to yourself?

Then HR gets shocked and speaks with a fake smile = Oh you are Rosella. I was just standing and now I should go. Bye.

After speaking this HR runs away from this place and Rosella speaks on seeing HR going away = this is a very strange boy.

Now HR comes far away from that place and speaks = Oh, this girl came again today to spoil my mind. Thankfully this girl did not see me in that computer class.

Then suddenly HR again gets a voice from behind him = Hey HR why have you been so nervous?

Then HR speaks in shock = I think you all will not let me live today.

Ravi = Who is not letting you live?

HR = None. You tell me when you came?

Ravi = Just now and how did you come to work so early today?

HR = That boss has sent me to learn computers and a new girl has started working in our office from today.

Ravi = oh so you were going to computer class right now?

HR = No, I was going to give this pen-drive to that new girl.

Ravi = Oh but HR, have you thought that this girl could be a spy of evil?

HR = Yes but I don't think that girl is a spy of evil.

Ravi = How can you say this, maybe she is hiding her true form. Let's see this pen-drive, maybe we can find some clues in this pan drive.

HR = Ravi, are you an international detective because of how much doubt you have.

Ravi = This is my job and now we go and see it in the computer shop.

HR = OK.

Now Ravi and HR go to the computer shop to see the files of this pen-drive.

HR = Hey Ravi, do you know how to run a computer?

Ravi = Yes and if you want, I can teach you.

HR = No thanks.

Ravi = This pen-drive has started.

HR = What is it in this pen-drive.

As soon as HR said this, Ravi speaks quickly = HR you close your ears and don't listen.

Now Ravi turns off the computer and HR asks Ravi = Ravi, what was it?

Ravi = It was a brainwash program and as I said, that girl works for evil.

HR = what? Okay, so we can go to that computer class and see what is happening there.

Ravi = Okay but first you should change your form using this ring.

HR = OK. **"Power Hidden"** turn me into a computer teacher.

Now HR and Ravi run to go that computer class and upon reaching this place, HR suddenly opens the door and speaks = Who is the head of this computer class?

Then everyone in the class looks at HR with a ghostly face and Ritika stands up and asks = What happened Sir? Is there an emergency?

HR = I can't believe you're running this evil, Ritika.

Ritika = I do not know what you are saying Sir and how do you know my name?

HR = Never mind, I see you in my true form.

## ~~ Lightning Of Fire Gives Me Power
## To End The Darkness ~~

# ~~ *Transform* ~~

Ritika = Rainbow Warrior.

Red warrior = oh, you know who am I.

Then suddenly Ritika's computer sir comes and grabs Ritika and says = Oh Ritika, I asked you to take care of computer class for a while, then you called this warrior.

Saying this, Ritika's computer sir turns into a demon.

Red warrior = Oh that means Ritika is not a demon. So, hey demon you let this girl go, because I am Rainbow Red Warrior. To destroy evil forces. To drive away the darkness. To erase evil from evil people. I have brought the power of truth and goodness. Listen, if evil people want to escape, then leave the evil, otherwise you will end with that evil.

Demon = It's time to check your files and you didn't make any of your files properly.

Red warrior speaks angrily = O...... you are not my boss and why should I make your files?

Demon = You have given the wrong answer and now you will be punished.

Saying this the demon attacks the red warrior.

Now the Red Warrior survives the demon's attack and goes to one of the corners of the class, and everyone in the class surrounds the Red Warrior, because the demon took control of all these people.

Demon = Hahaha.... Now Red Warrior you have only two choices. If you just give up now or you give up later.

Red warrior = I will never give up.

Now everyone slowly goes to the red warrior and the demon says = Is this your last answer?

Red warrior = Hay all of you stop now because I do not want to harm all of you.

Demon = Now it's your turn Ritika, I will control you and finish this warrior.

Now the demon tries to control Ritika forcefully but Ritika does not lose her control.

Demon = Don't fight with this strength and give me your Chi energy.

Ritika = I will not give you anything.

Ritika starts glowing in orange color by saying this and Ravi standing near the door sees that this is the second rainbow warrior.

Demon = Okay then you must die now.

Saying this the demon drops Ritika to the ground and as the demon go to die Ritika, suddenly Ravi throws a bracelet towards Ritika and says = Ritika, if you want to escape this demon then wear this bracelet. Say it out loud.

**~~ Wind of Storms gives me power to end the Darkness ~**

Ritika = Okay.

## ~~ Wind Of Storms Gives Me Power To End The Darkness ~~

## ~~ *Transform* ~~

Red warrior = O Ravi, help me because these people have come very close to me.

Ravi = Orange warrior quickly say this. (stormy wind)

Orange Warrior = OK. **[stormy wind]**

As soon as the orange warrior speaks, a sandstorm strikes, which is completely filled in the computer class.

Now the demon sees nothing and the power of this demon also starts to decrease, due to which the demon loses control of these people.

Orange Warrior = Red Warrior are you ok?

Red Warrior = Yes, now it seems to be my turn.

Saying this, the Red Warrior attacks this demon **[Lightning of Fire]** and this demon is destroyed at the same time.

Red warrior, Orange Warrior and Ravi see that everyone was

recovering, so all three go to some empty place.

**W**hen the trio reaches an empty spot, Ravi speaks = Hello Ritika, you are an Orange Rainbow Warrior. Are you happy?

Ritika = Yes, I am happy that I am a superheroine.

HR speaks surprised = what? Ritika, aren't you surprised?

Ritika = Why would I be surprised?

HR = Because all this will be new for you, therefore.

Ritika = No, because I learn a lot of new things, now I am not surprised. But I wondered how a coward like you became a warrior?

HR said angrily = O I am not a coward.

Ritika laughs and says = I am joking and I know that most of the hero's act like a coward in their human form to save their family.

Ravi = But Ritika, it is really a coward.

HR speaks again angrily = No, you are wrong Ravi and today you were also saying Ritika wrong.

Ritika = Okay, now stop fighting.

Now HR calm down and says with a smile = Okay, then Ritika you now know who I am, so now will you be make my files?...... :) :D :P :)

# (Chapter – 9)

The next day - Ritika teaches HR how to make files and HR gets bored learning this.

HR = Hey Ritika, don't you ever have fun?

Ritika = Fun? Like getting books or running a computer.

HR = No, not this. Never mind, you go with me tomorrow and Ravi will also be with us. Okay.

Ritika = Okay.

Here Darkness speaks to Victor = Victor, this time again your demon was destroyed by the hands of that warrior. But it is good that other warrior came out and maybe that all other warriors will come out from your new plans.

Victor = Thank you my boss and now I have another new plan.

Darkness = Okay then tell.

Victor = This time I will speed up the time of people. In this way, the Chi energy of all those people will increase manifold and this time I will throw those two warriors in the trap of my time, from which they will not be able to get out.

Darkness = very good. Go start this plan

Victor = As you wish my boss.

The next day HR, Ravi and Ritika, all three come to the mall, eat pizza, watch movies and more. In the evening, all three go to a park.

Ritika = Oh so now I came to know that we have to eliminate evil from the people of this earth.

Ravi = We can never destroy that darkness, so we should spread goodness in people as much as possible.

Ritika = Oh, Ravi but why are we called warriors and how many more warriors are there other than me and HR?

Ravi = All you warriors are 1,728,000 years old and that's why the hero who survived at that time was called a warrior.

HR is shocked to hear this and says = what! Are we so old?

Ravi = No, the one who is your soul is 1,728,000 years old and the one who is your body has taken birth again.

Ritika = Oh, so where are the other warriors?

Ravi = I don't even know that yet but you are all like Rainbows.

Then HR suddenly said = Hey, both of you, see that many people are gathered in the shop in front of the park. Let us also go there and see what is happening here.

Ravi & Ritika = Okay.

On reaching this shop, Ravi thinks in mind = I am feeling very bad energy from this place.

Ritika = This is shop of watches. Perhaps this shop is new open today.

HR = oh, wow look, the new types of watches are.

Ravi = I will take a watch.

HR = Why do you want a watch?

Ravi = just like that.

But Ravi thinks in mind = I doubt that these watches are the next step of evil.

HR = So I will also take a watch and Ritika, will you also take a watch?

Ritika = No, I already have.

HR = OK. So, I'll take a wall clock and an alarm.

Ritika = Ok, now I go. So, let's meet tomorrow.

HR = OK Good Night and Ravi, you have been silent, since we saw the clock?

Ravi = There is nothing like that. OK, Good Night.

HR = Good night.

Now HR comes home and gives the wall clock to his parents and goes to sleep setting the alarm in his room.

**T**he other side - Ravi sees this clock in his house and thinks what is strange in this clock. But Ravi does not understand anything and then goes to sleep. Now after midnight, when its clock is thirteen o'clock, then this clock starts glowing. Just then Ravi awakens with the glow of this clock and sees that the light was coming from this time and how thirteen o'clock time are happening in it.

The next day Ravi goes to HR's house early in the morning. When Ravi knocks at the door of HR's house, HR's mother comes.
Ravi = Hello aunt, did HR wake up?
HR's mother = He had gone to work a few hours earlier.
Ravi said in surprise = What, he left so soon.
HR's mother = OK son, now I also go because I have a lot of household work.
Ravi = Okay.
Now Ravi thinks in his mind = maybe that evil has taken over HR. Now I must find Ritika and get help from her.

Here many people had come early on HR's work.
Ajay = Now where is the boss.
HR = I have also eaten my lunch, but where is the boss?
Neha = How soon work is happening today.
The office worker says = Boss has coming.
Now everyone leaves the office by telling the boss that they are delayed in doing other things.
Then Steve stops everyone but nobody stops.

Other side, Ritika was still going to work, then it sees that all the people of the city are running here-there, hurrying.
Then, Ravi comes to Ritika and explains the whole thing.
Ritika = So what should we do now.
Ravi = Look at this clock to see what is wrong with it.
Ritika = But, will this evil spell work on me?
Ravi = Hold on, take this.
Ritika = what is it.
Ravi = this is a small pocket computer
Ritika = wow, that's very good. Okay, so now let's look at this

clock and see that this clock is pulling energy waves. Now let's open this clock.

When Ritika opens this clock, this clock is destroyed by glowing.

Ritika = what happened?

Ravi = This proves that there was an evil spell on this clock. Now we should hurry along with HR and go to that watch shop.

**O**n this side, all the people of the city were caught in the trap of time by this magic.

Now Victor speaks to his demon at the watch store = You have done a great job and Darkness is very happy to see this work.

Demon = Thank you my boss. This watch plan was good.

Victor = Now we have taken energy from a lot of people, that's why people are going crazy in the city and now you must be cautious because seeing all these things, those warriors will definitely come.

Demon = Don't worry, I am ready for those warriors.

Victor = Very good, now I am going to give some energy to Darkness and you wait for those warriors at this place.

**O**ther Side - Ritika and Ravi were tired of searching for HR but HR was not stopping at one place.

Ravi = Hey Ritika, let's go and see HR again in the café?

Ritika = Should we both go to that watch shop and end that evil?

Ravi = I do not think that this is right thinking because all those demons are slowly becoming stronger, that's why we should take HR with us.

Ritika = Okay, but where will HR be now?

**H**ere HR, like all the people of the city, was rushing to do his work quickly and on the run, HR does not know where he is and suddenly, he collides with Ritika and Ravi.

HR said angrily = O you go side by side.

Ravi = HR you.

HR = Hey Ravi, what are you doing at this place? Leave it, I don't have time.

Ritika = Wait HR, it's doing all evil.

Now Ravi tells the whole thing to HR. Then all three go to that watch shop.

Now after reaching this watch shop, HR stands in front of that watch shop, then quickly Ravi is at the side with HR and speaks to HR = what are you doing.

HR = I am going to end that evil.

Ritika = But HR cannot directly go inside us because the shop is closed now, so we will have to see some other way.

Ravi = Ritika is right.

HR said angrily = You are talking so much waste. We will go straight through the front door.

Ravi = You are very serious this time, but you should go as a warrior.

HR = OK.

## ~~ Lightning Of Fire Gives Me Power
## To End The Darkness ~~

## ~~ *Transform* ~~

Red warrior = Ritika, now you also transform quickly become a warrior.

Ritika = Okay.

## ~~ Wind Of Storms Gives Me Power
## To End The Darkness ~~

## ~~ *Transform* ~~

Ravi = I still feel that we are doing very quickly.

Red warrior = Oh you care so much. Now step back and see my awesome. **[Lightning of Fire]**

Now the attack of the Red Warrior hits the shop door, causing a big hole in that door.

Red warrior = Now we should go to that shop quickly.

Now these three runs towards that shop, but while going inside that shop, the hole of the shop door starts closing and Ravi is left outside this shop.

Ravi = Oh no, I should have run away quickly and now I am left outside this shop.

Orange Warrior = Hey Red Warrior Ravi left out.

Red warrior = Never mind we both can end this evil, just go with me. There is another door on that side.

Now as soon as the red warrior opens this door, only then he sees a big clock in front of him.

Now the voice comes from that clock = I was waiting for you, warriors.

Red Warrior = The time has come to end this evil because I am Rainbow Red Warrior.

Orange Warrior = And I am Rainbow Orange Warrior.

Both together = To destroy evil forces. To drive away the darkness. To erase evil from evil people. we have brought the power of truth and goodness. Listen, if evil people want to escape, then leave the evil, otherwise you will end with that evil.

Demon = what said time. Time will change now. If you have the courage and want to defeat me, then come to me in this clock. Hahaha......

Red Warrior = Let's go Orange Warrior.

Orange Warrior = Okay.

Now both come inside this clock but both of them are surprised to see that there are many doors inside this clock.

Red warrior = I have come in this watch, now you stop hiding and come out.

Demon = I am not hiding, just you have not come to me yet. Now you come to me.

Red warrior = Okay I'll chase your voice and come to you.

Orange Warrior = Wait, Red Warrior, let me check something.

Saying this, the Orange Warrior checks all the doors of this clock from her pocket computer and findings the demon.

Red warrior = what is it?

Orange Warrior = This is my pocket computer. Ravi gave me.

Red warrior = Oh but you are spending a lot of time. I can't wait any longer.

Saying this, the Red Warrior opens one of the doors and puts his foot in that room and then the age of the Red Warrior starts decreasing, then suddenly the Orange Warrior pulls it out, which makes its age normal.

Red warrior = what just happened to me?

Orange Warrior = This is a clock, so this demon has the power to control time and he really turn you into a child.

Red warrior = that means, it can make me old also?

Orange Warrior = Yes.

The red warrior now speaks with panic = Are we caught in its trap, oh no, who will save us now?

Orange warrior = You don't worry, Red warrior. I am looking for a way out of my pocket computer.

Red Warrior = So hurry up.

Orange warrior = I found it, that's the right door.

Red Warrior = Okay then come on.

Now both of them finally reach this demon.

Red warrior = now your game is over.

Saying this, the Red Warrior begins to attack then his body suddenly freezes.

Red warrior = what is happening, Orange warrior?

Orange warrior = I am also frozen, Red warrior.

Demon = You cannot spoil my plan at this place because it is my place. Now you are frozen because I have stopped your time and now the Chi energy of both of you is mine.

Both warriors get scared and shout = someone save us

Other side - Mysterious Girl comes through the window in this clock shop and sees that there is no one in this shop. Suddenly, the Mysterious Girl is heard screaming from a clock.

Mysterious Girl = This sounds like a red warrior and this voice is coming from this big clock.

Now the Mysterious Girl spends no time attacking the clock with her light beam which looks like a rose and this clock breaks.

**T**hen on this side, the demon inside the clock, loses its control by the power of time and at the same time it becomes a little week and the warriors were no more frozen here.

Red Warrior = O Orange warrior, see now I can move.

Orange Warrior thinks in her mind = This is the time to finish this demon.

By thinking this the Orange Warrior attacks the demon, **[stormy wind]** and the entire place is filled with sandstorms, this causes the demon's strength to decrease even further.

Orange Warrior = O Red Warrior, this is the right time to quickly attack that demon now.

Red warrior = OK... **[Lightning of Fire]**

Then the attack of the Red Warrior destroys the demon and this shop disappears and both these warriors come in their human form.

**N**ow Ravi meets HR and Ritika and speaks = You both did a great job and you know that Mysterious Girl broke that clock from the outside.

Red warrior said with a blush = What, Mysterious Girl had come.

Ritika = who is this Mysterious Girl?

Ravi = She has been helping HR from the beginning, defeating that demon and HR like that........

Even before this thing is completed, HR stops Ravi from speaking and says with blushing = what you are speaking, Ravi. Oh, look how long it's been, now I should go home. Good Night.

Then Ravi and Ritika are surprised to see HR going.......... (-- _ --)

<h1 align="center">(Chapter - 10)</h1>

Other side - Darkness = Victor This was your very good plan, but I am not happy with you because your demon was destroyed by the warriors again. Now I want to take complete control of this world but those warriors can stop me.

Victor = You don't worry my boss because I have another plan ready.

Darkness = Very Good and this time if both those warriors interfere in your plan, then finish them.

Victor = As you say, my boss and this time I will return only after killing those warriors.

Next day, HR and Ravi meet Ritika at the bus stand.

Ritika = Both of you are late.

Ravi = this is HR's fault because it is always late.

HR said with fake smile = sorry it will not happen again.

Ritika = I do not believe that I am going to take leave from work today and go to that carnival.

HR = Oh now let it go, just have fun.

Now these three go to the carnival on the other side of the city by bus. When these three arrive in this carnival, they see that there too much police at this place, then they go to the police to see why the police is so much at this place.

On reaching the police, Ravi asks = Sir, why is there so much police at this place?

Police Officer = Some people have disappeared from this place.

HR = How?

Police Officer = We don't know. Those people had going the

bus coming in the afternoon and evening and now there is no more question, go somewhere else.

Now all three of them go and talk somewhere.

Ravi = Both of you now be cautious as this may be the next step of evil.

HR = Oh you are worrying again.

Ritika = No HR, when both of you were talking to the police, I heard from the people running on the side that the bus had disappeared with the people.

HR = Oh Ritika you are also worrying. Stop worrying and look at that shop there, how crowded it is. Let's see what is in that shop.

After reaching this shop, HR said = Hey look, there are so many good fortunate things in this shop.

Ravi = HR, why are you taking this fortunate thing?

HR = That is the dream that I see while awake, i wish that dream comes true.

Ritika = I'll take one too.

HR = Hey Ritika, is there any person in your mind, that is why you are buying things of good fortune?

Ritika = No, I just want more information, that's why.

HR now said in shock = What, information. But how much more information does you want?

Ritika = as much as possible.

As soon as Ritika says this, suddenly a voice comes from behind HR = Do you want something good luck, handsome gentleman?

Then HR turns around and sees an old woman behind him.

Now HR was about to say something to that woman, then a boy comes from the shop and says = O grandmother, you are disturbing people again?

Old lady = Oh no son, I was just telling people about the things in our shop.

This boy = just enough. We run this shop only during carnival and festivals and even on this day, if you harass people, how will this shop run?

Ravi = How hard is this boy working. You too start working so hard, HR.

HR = Hard work will not suit me.

This boy suddenly feels something bad.

This boy = there is some evil power near this place. Wait I do something

Saying this, this boy starts praying with his eyes closed and his comes out Stemp of his pocket and moving his hand around, then suddenly his hand in which he has caught Stemp, this hand hits HR's face and HR falls unconscious.

This boy = oh no forgive me, it happened by mistake. Please bring it quickly to my house, my house is nearby and Grandmother, you must see the shop because I am taking this boy to my house.

Now this boy, Ritika and Ravi bring HR to this boy's house and then this boy goes to get hot water.

Ritika speaks in a panic = what will happen now, what will we do if HR doesn't wake up? This is all my fault; I should not have come to this place.

Ravi = Ritika, don't you panic, look HR will wake up now. Hey Look Mysterious Girl.

Then HR suddenly wakes up and speaks = Mysterious Girl, where is it - where is it?

Ritika = Oh HR, how foolish you are.

Now this boy comes into the room and speaks = Oh you have woken up. I'm sorry this happened by mistake. Are you ok now?

HR = Yes, I am fine no problem.

This boy = My name is Happy and I see the future in my mind.

HR and Ritika speak in shock = You can predict?

Happy = yes but that future is mostly wrong.

HR = Oh and I am Harvinder, but everybody calls me HR and this is Ravi and Ritika.

Happy = Hello, glad to meet you all.

Now Ravi speaks in his mind = I am feeling very strong energy from this boy.

Then the door is open and a man brings hot water.

This man = take sir hot water.

Happy = Okay thanks. Now you go and help Grandma.

This man = Okay.

After this man leaves, Ravi thinks again in his mind = This man's voice sounds familiar.

HR = Who was this man?

Happy = that Mr. V and they have been hired by grandmother today. Sometimes I think go away from this place, but there is no one to take care of my grandmother, that is why I am looking for some part time work.

HR = Never mind, everything will be alright. Let's go back to the carnival.

Now it all comes back to Happy's shop and Happy sees that there were a lot of people making noise at his shop. Then Happy asks this people = why are you all making noise?

Then one of these people said = We have come to know that when our relatives were coming home from the afternoon bus after buying good luck things from this shop, they all disappeared with that bus. That is why all this mistake is made of this good luck fortune things.

Now Happy spoke angrily = what are you saying. It is not yet known how those people have disappeared and you have also decided who is the thief? Stop this wrong accusation and go to the police and ask if they get those people or not. Now I want to tell all of you to go away.

Now HR, Ravi and Ritika go to the other side and discuss to each other.

Ravi = You both know I was feeling very strong energy from Happy.

HR = You just keep on worrying.

Ravi = No HR, both of you should go with me to see if the afternoon bus comes in the evening.

HR = But I want that good luck.

Ravi = HR, this is not the time to buy good luck. Do not forget that you are a rainbow warrior and you must first eliminate this evil.

HR said slowly = Okay let's go.

Now Ravi, HR and Ritika keep an eye on the bus stand and see that the afternoon bus arrives in the evening.

Ritika = We are seeing this, does that missing bus come again or not?

Ravi = Yes.

HR = Hey Ravi Look here, all these people have that good fortune.

Ritika = Look at the faces of these people, how tired all these people are.

HR = I also wanted one such fortunate thing.

Ravi = HR Look properly, these people are lost somewhere.

HR = I also must lose in my dreams, which I see in the day.

Ritika = See that bus is coming, is this same bus that is disappeared?

Ravi = Maybe it is the same bus and I think this bus will also make these people disappear forever.

HR said fearfully = What, missing forever.

Ravi = HR, stop being afraid and see the face of the driver properly.

HR = OK.

Now this bus stops at the bus stand and everybody gets into the bus.

Ritika = Let us go on the bus now.

HR said fearfully = No I will not go on this bus because I am scared.

Ravi tries to force HR into the bus and says = Stop being so scared and get on this bus.

But HR sits down in the bus stand chair and speaks with a crying face = I don't want to get inside this bus.

Seeing this, Ritika also gets down from this bus and then this bus leaves, but this bus disappears while leaving and all three are shocked to see this.

After disappearing, this bus reaches a strange place and this place no light everywhere.

Now the driver of the bus comes in its real form which is demon and speaks to itself = this plan of Victor is the best and in this place these people will sleep forever and as long as these people will keep sleeping, we take Chi energy will continue. Hahaha.......

**N**ext day - HR and Ravi again go towards that carnival, then HR speaks on the way = If Happy has his hand in all this, then we should first stop Happy.

Ravi = No HR, it is not sure that Happy has a hand in this and why Ritika did not come today.

HR = She has gone to work today to explain the reason for my leave and she will also come for a while.

Now both of them arrive at Happy's shop and HR speaks to Happy = Hey Happy, thankfully you here because I had to tell you one thing.

Happy = what happened HR?

HR = You know that what people are saying is true. everyone who bought that good fortune from your shop have disappeared with that bus.

Happy said angrily = Are you blaming me? you don't know, Grandma and I haven't sold any good luck things yet.

HR = But Happy I saw with my eyes the things of good fortune near the people who were going to the bus.

Happy said again in anger = stop blaming me and leave it now and never come back.

Now HR and Ravi go towards the bus stand.

**W**hen both of them leave Happy's shop, then Happy finds a bracelet on the ground and Happy picks up the bracelet and says = Who would have dropped such a beautiful bracelet. Never mind I wear this bracelet.

As Happy wears this bracelet, Happy gets Mr. V suspects and Happy sees Mr. V hiding, then Happy realizes that Mr. V is selling good luck things to everyone.

Now Happy calls Mr. V to his house and says = Now your game is over because I have seen everything and now you must go to the police station to confess your crime.

Mr. V = I do not think so because you will go to this dark place now. Hahaha.......

On saying this, suddenly a black circle becomes below Happy and Happy falls in this circle.

**O**ther side - HR and Ravi watch this bus stand to see if the bus comes again.

HR = Will we be sitting all day at this place.

Ravi = No because this time we will go in that bus.

HR = No I will not go in that bus.

Ravi = If you remain afraid like this, then everyone will call you a small child.

HR = OK but let me change into some other form first.

Ravi = Okay then hurry up because that bus is coming.

HR = OK **"Power Hidden"** Turn me into someone.

Ravi = Why have you turned into a postman?

HR = This is not the time to talk, let's go to the bus.

Now inside the bus, HR says = Bus driver your game is over now and now you go to the police station.

When HR says this, the driver starts laughing and this bus starts flying, then HR and Ravi fall on the back seat of the bus.

Here Ritika was coming to this bus stand, then Ritika noticed that this bus is start to disappearing, then Ritika runs to catch this bus but it disappears completely.

**N**ow this bus again reaches that strange place and the driver gets out of the bus and catches Happy and comes in his demon form.

HR said with a crying face = What, where am I? Maybe I disappear forever at this place.

Ravi = you stop crying and quickly turn into a warrior.

HR said while crying = No I am scared. **"Suddenly"** Okay so I'm becoming a warrior.

Ravi = Oh how soon you change your mind.
HR =

## ~~ Lightning Of Fire Gives Me Power
## To End The Darkness ~~

# ~~ *Transform* ~~

I am Rainbow Red Warrior. To destroy evil forces. To drive away the darkness. To erase evil from evil people. I have brought the power of truth and goodness. Listen, if evil people want to escape, then leave the evil, otherwise you will end with that evil.

Demon = This will not be happening.

HR = Oh really, then look it this.

The Red Warrior attacks by saying this. [Lightning of Fire] But this demon captures this lighting except Happy.

Demon = Have you bought a gift for me?

Red warrior speaks with Concentrated = Lightning of Fire, trap this demon.

Now the Red Warrior's attack becomes a rope and slows down the demon, then the Red Warrior goes to Happy and speaks = Happy, are you alright?

Happy = Who are you and how do you know my name.

Ravi = Happy, this is not the time to talk, you say this word quickly.

Happy = Hey, you are Ravi.

Ravi = Yes and after meeting you this morning I came to know that you are Yellow Rainbow Warrior, that's why I threw a bracelet with you. Now quickly you say this word aloud.

**~~ Stone of Weapons gives me power to end the Darkness ~~**

Red Warrior = What, Happy is a Rainbow Warrior?

Ravi = Yes and now speak quickly, Happy.

Happy = Okay.

## ~~ Stone Of Weapons Gives Me Power

## To End The Darkness ~~

# ~~ *Transform* ~~

On this side, the demon is freed from the attack of the Red Warrior and comes to attack all three. Then suddenly the Yellow warrior speaks = You have taken the wrong person. Now you face my missile.

The Yellow Warrior attacks by speaking it. **[Stone Missile]** Now this attack hits the demon and the demon is destroyed at the same time.

Red warrior = wow, what a tremendous attack.

Ravi = Hey look up there.

Red warrior = what is there?

Ravi = This black circle is the way to go outside and it is closing quickly.

Red warrior = What, is there no other way to go outside?

Ravi = No.

This side, it was night on outside so now Ritika prays that her friend and everyone else comes back safely, then suddenly the light comes out from Ritika's bracelet and slows down the circle.

On the other side Ravi sees this light and says this is the sand of the Orange warrior, which is slowing the time of this circle.

Yellow warrior = We must take all these people also.

Then a girl sitting on the bus seat says = Hello warriors, do you want to go my way?

Seeing this girl, the Red Warrior blushes and says = Mysterious Girl, you have come to save me from this place.

Yellow warrior = Do you like this girl or is there something else.

Ravi = Stop talking to both of you and see Mysterious Girl is taking these three buses along and now we should also hurry.

Now seeing all these coming back, Ritika becomes happy and

the Red Warrior speaks happily to Ritika = Hey Ritika, you saved our life.

Ritika = how is that possible?

Ravi = Ritika You have the power to slow down time.

Ritika = Oh.

Here Mysterious Girl speaks to herself = Now I should also go home.

Now as soon as the Mysterious Girl leaves, the Red warrior thinks = Oh I did not thank the Mysterious Girl at all, I will say it now.

When the Red Warrior goes to the bus to thank the Mysterious Girl, it sees that the Mysterious Girl had already left and sees that the Yellow Warrior has also come to see the Mysterious Girl.

Red warrior = what have you come to see? Oh; Hey have you also started to like Mysterious Girl?

Yellow Warrior blushes and speaks = No, I just came to thank her because she helped us a lot and would stop to say goodbye if she liked you.

Red warrior said with a crying face = what means, if? she does not like me???

**O**ther side - Victor speaks angrily to himself = warriors, you have survived this time but now I will see you tomorrow with my new plan....

## *(Chapter – 11)*

The next day at noon, Ritika and HR meet Ravi.

Ritika = Hey Ravi, today we have come to you again after taking a break from work because I saw in the news a while back that some people going to that carnival are doing very strange behavior.

HR = Ravi, maybe this could be the next step of evil.

Ravi = Oh so maybe you are right and it is very good that you are taking this warrior work seriously, HR.

HR said angrily = Hey, do you mean I was not serious before?

Ritika = stop fighting and let's go to that carnival and see what is wrong.

Now these three come to this carnival and after reaching this carnival, they all go to Happy.

Ravi = Hey Happy, how are you?

Happy = Hello I'm fine and how are you all?

Ravi = We are all fine also and now you are a rainbow warrior, then you have to go with us to eliminate evil.

Happy = Ok, so let's go but where are we going to go?

Ritika = Hey HR, what are you doing, why is your attention not here and what are you looking at in your phone?

HR = You all know that a girl is very famous nowadays with the help of internet.

Happy = what really, show me too.

HR = No I will not show you.

Happy = Hey, show me.

HR = No, I will not show you.

Ravi spoke angrily = Enough.

HR = But started by Happy first.

Ravi = HR Enough.

HR = OK.

Ritika = Ok, now all of you reduce your anger and let us all see what is going wrong in this carnival.

Happy, HR and Ravi = Okay.

There were many journalists gathered in the castle of carnival here and these journalists wanted to meet the person who running this carnival in the castle, but the castle's servant from the door tells this = the owner of this castle has said that in this carnival There is no mess and he will meet you all later.

Saying this, the servant of the castle closes the door of the castle and these journalists now leave this place.

Now this servant who is actually Victor, it speaks to itself = Those people do not know that I have laid trap to trap those warriors, because now it is three warriors, but this time I want those warriors completely I will finish it and I will take the energy of all the people who have come to this place. Hahaha.......

Other side - now these four were looking in this carnival to see what was wrong with this carnival then suddenly Ritika speaks = Hey guys where is HR?

Ravi said in surprise = What, HR is lost?

Happy = No, I saw him going towards that merry-go-round.

Now Ravi angrily speaks to HR = Hey HR, what are you doing, you don't know where we are?

HR = Don't worry, if we have come to this carnival then let's have some fun.

Ravi = No, we must do a very important job.

HR = But I want to have fun.

Happy = You will enjoy yourself because you are a child. Hahaha.......

HR angrily said to Happy = Wait, I will not let you go.

Saying this, HR comes near to catch Happy to fight Happy, but Happy starts running away from HR then suddenly Happy falls by running and HR gets scared seeing this and says = Hey Happy you Do not move because you have a wild bear.

Happy = Stop kidding, I'm alright.

Then Happy turns to look back and Happy is also scared to see this bear. Then a woman comes to these two in the clothes of the queen and tells to both of them = Do not be afraid both of you because it is a robot.

HR = what, a robot.

This woman = yes, and all the other animals are also robots of this carnival. Look at this

HR = wow and you are control these animals with this magic wand?

This woman = Actually this stick is a remote control.

Happy = Oh, I already knew.

HR = how big a liar.

Ravi = You two stop fighting.

Ritika = You are the queen of this carnival?

This woman = yes and after a while I will start a big party in the castle of this carnival and you all must come to this party.

Ravi = But why have you called us all in this party?

This woman = Because today is the last day of Carnival and everyone is coming to that party in this carnival.

Ravi, Ritika, HR and Happy spoke together = Oh, thank you.

Now after this woman leaves, Ritika speaks = Let us now see this carnival to see if there is anything wrong.

HR = But we have not seen even half this carnival and i have tired.

Ravi = Okay then we split up. With this, we can see this carnival quickly to see if there is anything wrong.

HR = What, should we split up?

Ravi = Yes, Ritika you come with me and you go with Happy.

Happy and HR spoke together = What, we both must go together?

Ravi = Come on, you two are together. Okay, so Ritika, let's go now.

Ritika = Okay guys, take care both of you.

Now after going to the other side of Ravi and Ritika, Happy speaks to HR = Ok HR, so now we should do our work as well.

HR = Okay but first you go with me in this Ferris wheel.

Happy = Oh no.

**N**ow after sitting on the Ferris wheel, Happy said = Why are we sitting in this children Ferris wheel.

HR = Because I am afraid of big Ferris wheel.

Saying this, HR is shocked to see the second compartment of this children's Ferris wheel and tell to the girl sitting in the second compartment of this children Ferris wheel = O Rosella, why are you sitting this children Ferris wheel?

Rosella suddenly looks at HR and says = Oh HR you are, but I also want to ask you, why are you sitting this children Ferris wheel?

HR spoke angrily = Hey I asked first.

Rosella = You got angry, Eye on Top.

Happy = HR Why is this girl calling you, Eye on Top.

Rosella = I tell you because it is a habit of daydreaming by looking upwards like children.

Happy = Oh yes, this name is good for its child's habit, Eye on Top.

Rosella = Yes, Eye on Top.

Now HR said loudly in anger = Enough, stop calling me by this name and now I am going.

Saying this, HR starts going then Happy comes to HR and says = Hey HR don't be angry, it was just a joke and you think this girl can be Mysterious Girl?

HR = What, Rosella? No, Mysterious Girl is so beautiful and good but this girl is bad and crazy.

As soon as he says this, Ravi's call comes on HR's phone and Ravi tells HR on the phone = Both of you should come quickly to this Castle.

Happy = what happened HR?

HR = Ravi called and he called us quickly towards the Castle.

Happy = Let's go quickly.

**H**ere the Queen of the Castle inside the Castle asks everyone = How did you like this fresh food?

Everyone says that this food is very good.

Queen of the Castle = very good, now you sleep.

When the Queen of the Castle says this, everyone starts sleeping slowly and there was also Ritika in the Castle who tries to wake up but it also falls asleep slowly.

**H**ere Victor speaks to himself in his secret place = Now all three warriors will come to save these people and when those warriors come, they will not escape from this demon. Hahaha.......

**N**ow approaching this Castle, HR speaks = O Ravi we arrived as soon as possible. Now say what is wrong.

Happy = Hey where is Ritika?

Ravi = She is inside.

HR = She didn't even wait for us?

Happy = I feel very bad energy from inside, I think the party is over.

Ravi = What? we should go in quickly and see if there is something wrong.

Happy = Okay, then first we should become warriors.

## ~~ Stone Of Weapons Gives Me Power
## To End The Darkness ~~

## ~~ *Transform* ~~

HR = I'm change also.

## ~~ Lightning Of Fire Gives Me Power
## To End The Darkness ~~

## ~~ *Transform* ~~

Now after making the warrior, the Yellow Warrior attacks the door **[Stone Missile]** and the door breaks and they enters.

After reaching inside, see that there is only the Queen of the Castle and the Red Warrior asks to the Queen of the Castle = Miss Queen, where is everyone?

Queen of the Castle = They are all resting in the other room and you must be tired too, please drink this power syrup.

Red Warrior = Oh thank you.

As soon as the red warrior starts drinking this syrup, then quickly the yellow warrior snatches the syrup from the red warrior and throws it somewhere. However, a little syrup falls on the yellow warrior's hand and making the yellow warrior's hand stone.

Red warrior said in a panic = Hey yellow warrior your hand.

Yellow warrior = Never mind I do something.

Saying this, the Yellow warrior speaks in the mind = power of stone, heal my hand.

Seeing this, the Red Warrior speaks = Thank goodness you are fine Yellow Warrior and thank you for saving me.

Yellow warrior = Never mind and now we must defeat this evil queen.

Queen of the Castle = Now I think it's time for the Queen to change.

Saying this, the queen turns into a robot girl and says = Hello I am a beautiful robot and will you play with me?

Seeing this, the red warrior speaks = wow, how beautiful is a robot.

Yellow warrior = You should probably say, bad robot.

Red Warrior = Oh yes, I am the Red Rainbow Warrior and your game is over.

Demon robot girl = game over, but the game has just begun.

Saying this, the Demon robot creates a mirage and they are trap in this mirage.

Ravi = both of you carefully. This could be trick of this robot.

Red Warrior = You say this to the Yellow Warrior.

Yellow warrior = Hey, I'm listening.

Red warrior = hey look, Mysterious Girl.

Ravi = No, this is not true.

Yellow warrior = I feel that truth.

Saying this, both of them go to the Mysterious Girl and Ravi speaks while stopping them = No wait this is a trap.

However, these two do not listen and start playing games by holding the hand of the Mysterious Girl.

Demon Robot = You two warriors have fallen into my trap and now I will die you both.

Then suddenly the light beam that looks like a rose comes and collides with the remote-control stick of the Demon robot and the stick is destroyed. Now these three are freed from this mirage.

Mysterious Girl = Hello warriors, now you cannot fall into the trap of this mirage. Now I am going.

Demon Robot = I will finish you later, Mysterious Girl.

Ravi said softly = O warriors, this is the right time, let us quickly find Ritika and finish this demon.

Both spoke together = Ok.

Now these three runs to find Ritika.

Demon robot = hey where are you three going?

Red warrior = You only said that we should play the game. So, we are running and you catch us.

Demon Robot = Okay and if I catch you then you will die.

Red Warrior = Okay.

Yellow warrior = what are you saying.

Red warrior = Never mind. We find Ritika.

Ravi = Let's go to this room.

Now after looking at some rooms, they find the room in which everyone was sleeping.

Ravi = Look at that, Ritika.

Red warrior = what has happened to it?

Yellow Warrior = Don't panic, it's just sleeping.

Ravi = O, wake up, Ritika.

Now Ritika slowly wakes up and speaks = Hey friends she is a demon, queen of the Castle.

Red warrior = we know.

Ravi = Come on Ritika now quickly you too become a warrior.

Ritika = Okay.

## ~~ Wind Of Storms Gives Me Power To End The Darkness ~~

## ~~ *Transform* ~~

Ravi = She is coming.

Orange Warriors = Are We Ready Warriors?

Both warriors spoke together = Yes.

Saying this, the Orange Warrior attacks **[stormy wind]** and the room is completely covered with fog of sand and the demon's power begins to wane.

Demon robot = what is happening, why my power is decreasing. Now I must finish these warriors quickly.

Suddenly the red warrior speaks in the fog = You are looking for someone?

Orange Warrior = Attack you both quickly.

Now the Yellow Warrior attacks **[Stone Missile]** and then the Red Warrior attacks. **[Lightning of Fire]**

Now the Red Warrior attack has made this Yellow Warrior missile very powerful and then this missile goes and collides with the demon robot girl and then this demon is destroyed.

Ravi = You three have done a great job and now these people are awakening slowly and we should now go from this place.

The three said together = Ok.

**O**ther side - Victor was sending the power to this demon robot in his secret place because Victor wanted to kill these warriors by making this demon robot more powerful, but when Victor's demon robot girl is destroyed, Victor speaks to himself = Oh no, you warriors, you have also destroyed this demon of mine. I hate you warriors and now I must go to Darkness with this bad news.

Nooo..........

**N**ow the other side - Ravi = All three of you have done wonders and now even if you all fight together; no demon can defeat you.

HR = Oh thank you Ravi but are you listening, Happy.

Happy = hey you said something to me "Eye on Top"?

HR said angrily = Do not call me by this name.

Happy = I will call you "Eye on Top"

Now HR angrily runs away to catch Happy but Happy runs away from this place.

Ravi = Oh, when will these two improve? (--_--)

## (Chapter – 12)

The next day, HR was late again to go to work and after arriving at work, he sees that Ritika has been sent by the boss for some work outside the city.

Then HR speaks in his mind = I wish I could go on a vacation outside the city somewhere.

**H**ere the other side Victor was upset and speaks to himself = How do I get in front of Darkness because I have failed many times to die these warriors and this time Darkness does not give me another chance.

As soon as he says this, a girl comes to him with magic and this girl was actually a demon and likes Victor.

Victor = What are you doing here, Veronica?

Veronica smiles and speaks slowly = Victor, you are very angry today. What happened, are you not able to kill those warriors?

Victor = Have you come to this place to make fun of me?

Veronica = No Victor, I have come to tell you that Darkness probably needs me now.

Victor = very good, then you go to the Darkness.

Veronica = You did not understand. I said that now I help you to kill those warriors, but first we give that thing to the Darkness, which will make the Darkness happy.

Victor = What do you mean?

Veronica = First we will take a lot of Chi energy from people and give it to Darkness, then Darkness will give you more time so that you can kill those warriors.

Victor = But how will this happen?

Veronica = I have a plan.

Victor = Okay tell me.

Now Veronica tells Victor the plan and Victor is happy to hear this plan and says = Now it seems that those warriors will die. Hahaha.........

**N**ext day - HR goes to work and sees that Ritika has not come to work even today and then he goes to Ajay and asks Ajay = Hey Ajay, do you know when Ritika will come back to work?

Ajay = Why, have you started liking Ritika?

HR = Oh no, she is my friend just like you are and I was just asking that she can help me in making some files.

Ajay = Oh.

Then Neha comes to them and asks = Hey guys, what are you talking about?

HR = I wanted to know when will Ritika come back and make my files?

Neha = Oh, you don't know that Ritika will come back this evening.

Ajay = How do you know this?

Neha = Because when the boss sent her, she went to meet me and told her the time to come back.

HR = OK.

Neha = And you know that yesterday I was watching a contest on TV, in this we can ride a cruise ship for free for the whole day.

HR = Really?

Neha = Yes and a lot of people have won it but there are last two tickets left which will be drawn in a lucky draw right now.

Now HR runs away quickly after hearing this, because it wanted to win that ticket and after reaching this contest shop, it sees that there is a lot of crowd at this shop because many people came to win this contest, but this defeat Does not believe and goes ahead somehow.

Now many people had tried but could not win, now it is HR's turn and when HR tries his luck then it also cannot win.

Now HR starts leaving this place with disappointed, then suddenly someone calls HR = Hey HR what are you doing at this place?

HR looks at this person and speaks = Oh hello Happy, you heard about this contest? In this we can win a cruise ship ride for free for a day.

Happy = Yes, I heard.

HR = So you try one because only one person can try only once and I could not win.

Happy = Oh, okay move, I try.

Now Happy tries his luck by speaking something in his mind and it wins this contest.

Shopkeeper = Congratulations, you have won two tickets of the cruise ship leaving tomorrow morning and this ship will make you travel all over the sea by evening and you will also be able to enjoy the party in this ship. congratulations.

Now seeing this, HR speaks in his mind = how big cheater it is, it won the contest using its power. It should be disqualified.

**N**ow both go to a park and on arriving at this park HR speaks = Hey Happy, won't you take me on this cruise ship?

Happy = No.

HR = But why not, do you want to take a girlfriend?

Happy = No.

HR = Oh yes if you don't have a girlfriend then maybe you will go with your grandmother.

Happy said angrily = No.

Then Ravi and Ritika come to this park, searching for both.

Ravi = What have you two been doing in this park?

HR = Thankfully Ravi you have come and now you tell Happy that we warriors should live together.

Happy = oh that's good idea. Ritika, you will go with me on the cruise ship because I have won two tickets for the cruise ship leaving tomorrow morning.

Ritika = me, but you go away with HR.

Happy = No, you did not understand me. Let me tell you on the other side.

Now Happy takes Ritika to the other side and says = I cannot take HR as he starts to do like children.

Ritika = Oh, okay I go with you.

Happy = very good, I am sure we will have a lot of fun on that cruise ship.

But on this side HR was listening in secretly.

Now HR speaks in his mind = Happy thinks that I am left behind but I will go on this cruise ship somehow.

**N**ext morning - seeing the many people coming on the cruise ship, Victor speaks to Veronica = this is a very good plan. With this, we can take Chi energy of many people.

Veronica smiles and says = the warriors will not come to this sea and will not be able to escape if they come.

Victor = You're right because it is not a common ship. Actually, this whole ship has been built to take energy and now you can see that if everyone has come, then they take this ship into the sea.

Veronica = As you say, Victor.

**N**ow everyone was boarding this ship. Happy and Ritika were also on this ship.

But other side, HR was watching them from a little distance with Ravi.

Ravi = Why have we come to see them both at this place and you did not go to your work today.

HR = No, I have taken leave today and I am going on this ship.

Ravi = How is that possible?

HR = Look at this ring.

Ravi = No HR This is just to dodge evil.

HR = You start worrying again? Nothing will happen to me and now you stop worrying.

Ravi = No HR.

HR = **"Power Hidden"** Turn me into a journalist.

Ravi = You do not want to be improved.

HR = No and now let's go to that ship.

Now both go on this ship, but before going ahead on the ship, they are stopped by the security guard and HR goes ahead after seeing the ID of his journalist, but Ravi is unable to go further, now Ravi tells HR Take care and HR alone proceeded on this ship.

**N**ow Ritika, Happy and HR "who is as a journalist" were having a lot of fun on this cruise ship.

Ritika = Hey Happy, how much are you eating?

Happy = Hey, no problem because all this is free for us.

Ritika = But everyone is watching us.

Happy = Let it be seen and you also eat. Oh yes, I have an idea, can we take some pictures?

Ritika = But why.

Happy = that I will burn HR by showing this picture.

Ritika = No Happy it would be wrong.

Happy = Never mind, let's find a cameraman with me.

Ritika = Oh no.

**O**ther side - HR roams on this ship and reaches the deserted place of this ship and upon reaching this place it says to itself = I don't know which place I have come and they both of them have not met me yet. Oh, I should have brought Ravi with me somehow.

When saying this, suddenly a girl asking to HR from behind = What are you doing here? You do not know this is a restricted area on the ship.

Then HR sees this girl and says = Sorry Madam but I was lost with my friends and I could not find my way back. However, who are you, ma'am?

This girl = My name is Veronica and I am the second captain of this ship.

HR blushes and speaks = Oh wow, a beautiful and young girl like you is the captain of this ship. I cannot believe.

Veronica blushes and speaks = Oh are you telling the truth? But do you have a ticket?

HR = My ticket is with my friends and you are insulting my praise by talking about the ticket. Because I am right, you are a truly beautiful beauty.

Veronica is very shy and speaks = You are very good. Will you have dinner with me

HR = Sure.

Veronica = Okay, so now I meet you at tonight's dinner.

HR = as you say.

Now Veronica goes to the first captain's room "which is the first captain Victor." And here HR thinks = chasing this Veronica and see what she is doing in the first captain's room.

Victor = Why are you so happy? Oh, I get it. You are happy that this time our plan is working and this time those warriors will not come.

Veronica = No, but you are also right and now I can see that on which side you are collecting the Chi energy of all these people?

Victor = Yes. See this, the energy of all these people is being collected in this glass ball.

Veronica = wow, now by calling these people in the hall of this ship take out all the Chi energy of all the people at once and control these people, by this we will order all these people that the people of the city Also brought on this ship, which will give us more Chi energy.

Victor = you're right, Hahaha.......

On this side HR outside the cabin is surprised to see this and speaks to himself = Oh no, this ship captain works for evil. Now what should I do, I should have brought Ravi with me. Now I must first find Happy and Ritika and then stop these people.

Now HR finds Ritika and Happy in this ship. But on this side, Victor and Veronica make an announcement on the entire ship that everyone should come to the hall of this ship. HR also listens to this announcement and thinks in his mind = Oh no, the bad work of these evil people is about to begin. I should find Happy and Ritika quickly.

On this side, when everyone reaches the hall, Victor says = Hello friends, thank you all for coming to this ship and now the second captain of this ship will show you something.

Veronica now smiled and said = Thank you sir, now all of you look at this glass ball and see how your energy comes to me.

As soon as she speaks, it extracts the energy of all the people and everyone faints. Then Victor and Veronica see that two of these people are still fine.

Veronica speaks in surprise = this two people are still fine, how? Who are you both?

Both these people are Happy and Ritika and Ritika speaks = what are you doing this and what has happened to all these people.

Happy = Wait Ritika, I find these people bad and these people have taken away the energy of all these people.

Veronica = You're right.

Victor = Never mind, now we will make these two our slaves.

As Victor speaks, Veronica makes water monsters with her power and the monsters surround to capture Happy and Ritika, then Ritika screams with fear and the sound is heard by HR.

Hearing this voice, HR speaks to himself = This voice sounds like Ritika's. I think Ritika and Happy are in danger and that voice probably came from the hall of this ship. Now I must first become a warrior and then I go to help these two.

## ~~ Lightning Of Fire Gives Me Power To End The Darkness ~~

## *~~ Transform ~~*

**O**ther side - Victor speaks to Veronica = You now make these people your slaves and I go to give this energy to Darkness.

As soon as Victor says this, the door of the hall suddenly opens and the sound comes = You are hiding in this place.

Victor = Now who has arrived?

Red Warrior = I am Rainbow Red Warrior. To destroy evil forces. To drive away the darkness. To erase evil from evil people. I have brought the power of truth and goodness. Listen, if evil people want to escape, then leave the evil, otherwise you will end with that evil.

Veronica = yes-yes, your speech is enough. Now it's time for you to die.

Speaking of this, Veronica forcibly captured the Red Warrior and takes him to the deck of the ship.

Here Ritika speaks = Oh no, the Red Warrior is in danger.

Happy said in anger = Why and how did he come to this place?

Victor tells his water monster to hold both people and then Victor goes outside to see that Veronica is finishing that warrior?

On the deck Veronica change into her demon form and attacks with her power with tentacles of water.

Red warrior = Oh no, it can control the whole sea. I must defeat it quickly or else I will get into trouble.

Veronica = It's too late, Red Warrior. Now you will not be saved from dying.

Victor = Very good, you finish this warrior, Veronica.

Saying this, she attacks and before its attack is complete, the Yellow Warrior missile arrives and strikes the ship's deck.

Victor = You have also come.

Red warrior = Thankfully you became a warrior and finished those monsters.

Orange warrior = now quickly finish Veronica first.

Then as soon as she speaks, the Orange Warrior attacks **[Stormy Wind]** and her attack makes sand fog, which reduces Veronica's strength.

Now the Yellow Warrior attacks first quickly **[Stone Missile]** and then the Red Warrior makes his attack to make Yellow Warrior attack more powerful **[Lightning of Fire]** and this attack strikes Veronica and at the same time Veronica is destroyed.

Here Victor sees it and speaks angrily = Enough. You warriors have made me very angry. Now I will kill you all.

As soon as he said this, Victor was about to attack these warriors, that suddenly a sound was heard to all of them = Victor, you are not giving me any answer, what happened?

Victor = **"Darkness"** My boss I'm just going to finish these warriors.

Darkness = No, I am very angry right now because you are not obeying me, that's why you come to me now and then I will think whether you can finish these warriors or not.

Victor = My boss as you say.

Saying this, Victor tells these warriors before leaving = You have survived this time warriors, but if I get a chance again, I will finish all of you warriors.

Saying this, Victor disappears from this ship and takes some of the energy of all these people with him and this ship turns into a rusty ship and slowly starts going shore.

Now this warrior comes in his human form and Ritika says = Who was the captain of this ship?

HR = He was Victor. He is the master of all these demons and i think that he also has a boss who is even more powerful.

Ritika = Oh, so now we must make our powers more powerful.

Happy = that's fine but how did you get on this ship?

HR = This is a secret.

Ritika = Now both of you don't start fighting again and see that all these people are getting well and we have now reached the shore.

**N**ow these three meet Ravi.

Ravi = How did this ship become so rusty?

Now these three tell the whole story to Ravi and after hearing this story Ravi speaks = Oh, now all three of you must be more powerful.

Ritika = I said the same thing.

HR = Happy listening to this?

Happy = I am listening but next time I will take Mysterious Girl on a cruise ship.

HR speaks angrily = that girl will not go with you.

Happy = Just tell me why she won't go with me, do you love her?

HR = No.

Ravi = When will you both grow up?

Ritika = Ravi, saying them will do nothing.

Ravi = Okay let's go home now.....

<h1 style="text-align:center">(Chapter – 13)</h1>

The next day - Darkness = Victor, you have taken away the Chi energy of many people so that we can become more powerful, but despite using this energy, you have failed many times to defeat those warriors.

Victor = But my boss......

Darkness said angrily = silent, I give you one last chance and this time you will not send any of your demons, because this time you will go yourself to die those warriors. Now this time you will come back after killing those warriors, otherwise if you fail this time also, I will kill you. now go.

Victor thinks in mind while leaving this place = warriors, you will definitely die this time.

Now in the evening HR is coming to his house with Ravi.

HR = Ravi, do you think Mysterious Girl likes me?

Ravi = What are you saying, HR. You are the leader of this powerful warriors and you should think seriously.

HR = Don't give a speech like you are elderly and I think Ritu is probably a Mysterious Girl.

Ravi laughed and said = how silly you are, you keep thinking like children.

HR = Ravi, you don't say that to me.

Ravi = Okay, so now your house has come, so I will meet you tomorrow and we will see how all of you warriors can make your powers more powerful.

As Ravi speaks, suddenly the image of Victor appears on the sky and looking at this image, HR said = Hey Ravi, looking there, Victor's image is arrived in the sky.

Ravi = Oh no, I think it will be Victor's new plan to spread his evil.

Now Victor speaks by his image = Warriors, you have not left any other way with me, so now I challenge you that you all come and meet me near the shipyard after 12 o'clock tomorrow, otherwise I will destroy this city and look at this sample.

Saying this, Victor sets the city on fire.

Seeing this HR gets scared and Ravi speaks = Oh no, what did he do.

Now after the disappearance of this fire, Victor speaks = It was just an illusion and if you don't come then it will be true tomorrow. Hahaha......

Ravi = Oh no, HR you now go and rest and meet me at Happy's Place tomorrow after work.

HR = Okay good night.

Next day, everywhere in the city there was news that what was on the sky last night, what was that?

Now in HR's office, Steve speaks to his employees = Don't be afraid all of you and there is no need to take care of this and now you do your work properly.

After saying this Steve goes to his office room and Ajay & Neha come to HR and talk.

Ajay = Hey HR, what do you think, should we go to that place tonight?

HR speaks in shock = No.

Ajay = Why, are you scared?

HR = No, there is no such thing. I am just saying why we got into this trouble.

Neha = HR is right. Maybe it could be an attack by some external creatures who have come to occupy our earth.

HR thinks in his mind = Oh, Neha said it right.

Ajay = Neha, you just think in your thoughts. Does, anything like this happen?

HR = Yes, she's right and now we should not focus on this and do our work properly.

Ajay = Hey HR, you are speaking like a boss. Are you feeling well?

Neha = Yes, you are right Ajay.

HR said angrily = I'm fine, let me do my work.

Ajay = Okay don't be angry. Come on, Neha, let us do our work.

**N**ow HR goes to Ritika and tells her the whole story.

Ritika = Ok HR We will go together at Happy's place.

HR = No Ritika, you go alone because I must go somewhere else and then I will come from that place to Happy's place.

Ritika = Okay, but take care of yourself.

**W**hen HR is discharged from work, So HR goes to Ritu and narrates today's news.

Hearing this news, Ritu laughs and speaks = HR, how much do you think in your thoughts. I just like the fact that you are so cute, just like a child.

HR = Oh really? I should tell this to my friends.

Saying this, HR runs to Happy's place and on the way, HR collides with a girl.

Now HR speaks on seeing this girl = Rosella you, why do you come in my way again and again?

Rosella speaks angrily = You bump into me "Eye on Top".

HR also speaks angrily = How many times should I tell you don't call me by this name.

Rosella = Okay, but where are you going so fast?

HR smiles and speaks = I am going to tell my friends that I have been called cute by a girl.

Rosella says laughing = she would be crazy.

HR = All girl is not like you because she called me cute like a child.

Rosella = she rightly said that you are a child and just think that she considers you a child.

Now HR speaks sadly = You may be right but your words made me sad.

Speaking of this, HR starts crying and many people on the way look at them and speak to each other = See this, a girl made a boy cry.

Other person = Yes, this is the first time that a girl is making a boy cry.

Rosella = Hey HR, stop crying because people are watching us.

But HR does not stop crying.

Now Rosella speaks nervously = Ok HR…… So now I go my way. We will probably meet again. Bye.

Seeing this, Rosella leaves this place and seeing this, HR stops crying and starts going to Happy's place.

Now when HR reaches Happy place, Ravi speaks to HR = Oh HR you have come. Well, now all three of you listen that the time has come to stop the victor because all three of you are rainbow warriors, then all three of you will have to do this work.

Happy = Ravi, you are right and this time we will eliminate his evil or his.

Ritika = No, it can be a trap.

Happy = it's okay Ritika because we have no other way.

Ravi = You are right Happy and what will you say HR?

HR = what shall I say.

Ritika = Hey HR seems depressed.

Happy = Oh, it seems that some girl has broken HR's heart.

HR speaks in his mind = how can it be so right?

Ravi = Enough! Happy, stop joking because this is a very serious situation.

HR = Ravi, never mind. I was just thinking how to defeat Victor.

Ravi speaks in surprise = Hey HR, your health is fine because today you are speaking very seriously?

HR = I am fine and you only said that I should be serious. So now let's go to defeat Victor.

Ravi = Yes, let's go.

Now these four's start going towards that shipyard.

Other side - some policemen were standing on the shipyard

because the townspeople were scared after that threat from Victor. That is why some policemen are standing at this shipyard to protect the people.

11:30 pm Victor comes to this shipyard and sees that there are some policemen at this place.

Seeing these policemen, Victor speaks to himself = very good I have found some people who will help me in finishing these warriors and now I should control these policemen. Hahaha......

**O**n this side, Ravi, HR, Ritika and Happy were standing at the bus stand for an hour and were waiting for a ride that would take them that shipyard.

Happy = The day after the lockdown of Corona, all rides have stopped after 10 pm.

Ritika = Yes and no people are visible on the street also.

Now there were only two minutes left at midnight, then HR speaks on seeing a bus = Hey guys, see that a bus is coming this way.

Ravi = How can the bus come at this time.

When the bus reaches this bus stand, it is seen that there is no person in this bus and this bus has come on its own.

Happy = Maybe Victor has sent the private bus.

Ritika = I am speaking, this is definitely a trap.

HR = Never mind, let's go and see what Victor wants.

Ritika = But how did Victor send this bus to this bus stand? Does Victor know who we really are?

Ravi = Not at all, perhaps Victor would have sent many buses to many bus stands and no one would board this bus due to Corona's lockdown. That is why we will go on this bus and then Victor will know that all the warriors are coming to him. So that's why now all of you become warriors quickly and walk through this bus to Victor.

**Ritika = Okay.**

## ~~ Wind Of Storms Gives Me Power To End The Darkness ~~

## ~~ *Transform* ~~

**Happy = Okay.**

## ~~ Stone Of Weapons Lightning Of Fire Gives Me Power To End The Darkness ~~

## ~~ *Transform* ~~

**HR = OK.**

## ~~ Lightning Of Fire Gives Me Power To End The Darkness ~~

## ~~ *Transform* ~~

Ravi = Okay then let's go.

**N**ow all of them arrive at this shipyard and see that there are some policemen at this place.

Yellow warrior = Let's talk to them and ask what all these people are doing at this place late night.

Red warrior = what crazy you are. Wouldn't he ask you the same thing?

Yellow warrior = Hey, you shut up and let me ask.

Saying this, the Yellow Warrior summons these policemen and all the policemen come to them with a shout. Then all of them start running on the other side in fear.

Orange Warrior = Why are all these policemen following us?

Red warrior = don't know and you didn't see that the eyes of those policemen were glowing.

Ravi = It seems that this too is under the control of Victor.

Yellow warrior = what should we do now?

Red warrior = We must think quickly, because we cannot harm these people, because there is no fault of these people.

Orange Warrior = I do something. I see from my rainbow mini laptop that there is a way to heal these people.

Ravi = Okay then you continue this fight and I will see from afar how you all win this battle.

Red warrior = Why Ravi, won't you help us?

Ravi = No, I can only teach you how to fight because I am a servant of you all and I am not even a rainbow warrior.

Yellow warrior = Okay, then you go to the other side and let us face this trouble.

Now the Orange Warrior looks at these policemen on her laptop and says = Hey guys this is not a real policeman. However, Victor created these people with Chi energy of real policeman and if we eliminate these fake policemen then this chi energy will go back to real policeman.

Yellow warrior = Okay, then I do this work. **[Stone Missile]**

When all the fake policemen are destroyed, then Victor comes in front of them.

Victor = Very Good, Rainbow Warriors. All three of you have come at the right time as I wanted.

Orange Warrior = Oh no, was that its trap?

Victor = You warriors have done a lot to spoil my Plans and now we are enemies, so now you will die in this youth.

Red Warrior = Oh no, a handsome boy who has not yet seen the world and who has yet to propose many girls. He will die now?

Yellow warrior = which boy are you talking about?

Red warrior = my own, look at my face how handsome it is.

Yellow warrior = Yes, your face is just like a monkey.

Orange Warrior = Enough, both of you have forgotten why we are here.

Victor = Enough is enough, here you all have not come to talk. You all fight with me or die.

Saying this, Victor prepares the shipyard's fighting ships to kill these warriors and all these ships attack these warriors with their weapons. Now these warriors talk to each other while avoiding the weapons of these ships.

Orange Warrior = What shall we do now?

Red warrior = I don't know.

Yellow warrior = You don't worry, I finish these ships with my missiles.

Orange warrior = No; wait, if you do this, the weapons of these ships will spread throughout the city. This can put the people of the city in danger.

Yellow warrior = what should we do now?

Red warrior = There is only one way, run to save our life.

Other side – Victor was laughing looking at this scene and suddenly a ray of light "that looks like a rose" passes it near Victor's face, causing Victor's attention to wander. Then these fighting ships stop attacking.

Victor = Oh, you are very good, who came for me, Mysterious Girl.

Mysterious Girl = How do you know my name?

Victor = I know a lot.

Mysterious Girl = Ok Victor, so you are using the power of your magic to control the people of these worlds. This is very wrong.

Victor = So now I must learn from you what is wrong and what is right?

Mysterious Girl = If you want, I can teach you.

Victor = Enough, fight with me.

Saying this, Victor starts boxing with the Mysterious Girl, but both accidentally fall into the water in the middle of the fight and Victor comes out of the water with his magic and the Mysterious Girl when not out of the water, so the warriors are convinced that she may have died.

Now all these warriors are shocked to see this and Victor again attacks the warriors with the weapons of these shipyard ships.

Now again, these warriors talk among themselves while avoiding these attacks.

Yellow warrior = what should we do now because now it seems that Mysterious Girl is dead.

Red warrior = No, it cannot happen.

Orange Warrior = Hey guys I think this ship is attacking because of its radar and I have an idea.

Yellow Warrior = Speak fast?

Orange Warrior = I attack first and the two of us disappear from the radar of this ship and hide behind Victor, so that Victor's attack will come back on him.

Red Warrior = This is a very good idea, but who will be the one who will face these missiles?

Orange Warrior = You.

Red Warrior = Yes, of course. "Now say by shocked = what?" No, it will not be from me.

Yellow warrior = Why not, you got the power of warrior before us, that's why you have more experience than us to avoid attacks.

Red Warrior = Okay.

Orange Warrior = Okay. **[stormy wind]**

Now the fog of sand spreads everywhere with the attack of the Orange Warrior and the Red Warrior alone speaks to himself when facing these missiles = Hey guys, hurry up because I will not be able to escape these missiles anymore.

Victor gets nervous seeing this fog and says angrily = Oh no, this fog cannot spoil my plan.

Orange Warrior = Look at this side, Victor.

Victor = You did so wrong, Orange Warrior.

Orange warrior = Now you know what is wrong and what is right.

As the Orange Warrior speak this, the Yellow Warrior makes a mark of bad luck on Victor's back with the power of his luck and this mark has more effect on the evil people.

Now due to this mark the missiles of the fighting ships attack Victor and now Victor avoids these missiles by himself.

Now the fog is disappeared and these three warriors stood together.

Victor = You can't beat me.

Yellow warrior = now you have lost this battle, Victor.

Orange warrior = Now you will get, what you deserve.

Red warrior = Now this bad work for you will end forever and now is the time to punish you. **[Lightning of Fire]**

Now Victor survives Red Warrior's attack, but surviving Red Warrior's attack, he collides with the missiles of these fighting ships and then Victor is greatly injured.

Victor = No, I cannot defeat by you, warriors.

Saying this, Victor disappears from this place and now all the rainbow warriors meet Ravi and say = Hey Ravi, it seems that the Mysterious Girl is no longer in this world.

Ravi = Yes, I saw how Mysterious Girl fell into this water while saving you.

**O**ther side - Victor approaches Darkness in an injured condition.

Darkness = Victor You have lost again and now you know what punishment you will get.

Victor = But my boss, now I know how to find the true form of those warriors. Please give me one more chance.

Darkness said angrily = Shut up, you have got many opportunities. Now stop making excuses and now all the demons who work in this place should know what I do with them if they fail.

Victor speaks fearfully = No my boss, I beg you, don't do this........

As Victor speaks, Darkness destroys Victor.

Darkness = Now all of you demons have come to know that if any of you failed, then you too will be destroyed. Now tell who will come in place of Victor and who will finish those warriors?

As soon as the darkness is spoken, a girl speaks in the dark = Now I will do this work, my master.

Darkness = very good and if you have failed, then you know what will happen to you.

This girl = yes, my master and you do not worry because now all those warriors will die with my hands.

Darkness = very good. Hahaha.......

"What, Mysterious girl is still alive?"

"If Mysterious Girl is alive then what will these warriors know who is Mysterious Girl?"

"Which girl has now replaced Victor and is it more powerful than Victor?"

**This chapter will continue............** ☺

*Now we will meet in the next Volume. I hope you enjoy this story. Now you comment me on the photo of the cover of this book on Instagram if you want the next Volume as soon as possible?*

**Thank You. ��**

**Have a Nice Day ��**

~~~~~~~~~~~~~~~~~~~~~

H.S. Sandhu

~~~~~~~~~~~~~~

~~~~~~~~~

~~~~~

~